A DARING PLAN AND A COLD SHOULDER

BONE KNIGHT
BOOK 5

TIM PAULSON

Cover design and internal illustrations by Mark Smith Illustration

First Edition: May 2021

Ikkibu publishing

Created with Vellum

OTHER WORKS

Arcane Renaissance series:

Path of Ruin

Betrayal at Goliath Gate

Wrath of the Risen God

Bone knight series:

A Grim Demise and Even Worse Resurrection

A Doomed Fight and Not So Great Landing

A Hard Truth and An Unwise Decision

A Lost God and A Hostile Land

A Daring Plan and A Cold Shoulder

An Agonizing Day and A Dread Knight

An Impossible Task and A Vile Solution

A Brutal Clash and A Bitter Rival

A Grave Threat and Ultimate Illumination

Join Tim's mailing list at www.paulsonwriter.com and receive a free Arcane Renaissance novella.

1

WILDS AND WORRIES

"What are you doing?" Trina asked, her mouth hanging open.

Max looked down at his bones as he stepped down the cargo ramp at the back of their airship.

"Oh... sorry," he said as he pulled up his equipment menu, selecting the only available choice: the same dark leather he'd been wearing only a few minutes before. "I have to take off all my equipment in order to change my class."

"Yeah? Well, couldn't you have done that inside?" she replied.

Max crossed his arms. He didn't even feel embarrassed about it. He didn't have skin or organs. What was the point?

The good news was that the switch to Scavenger left him with the lightest headache so far, though once again he was back to a low skill level, just two, and his stats sucked. That didn't matter though, he hadn't changed for the combat prowess, but for the abilities.

While they'd been flying west, Max had dug into both of the guides he'd acquired from Trina's old school. They went into much greater depth than Khilen's little listing, including possible upgrade paths. The first guide was for Rogue, which it turned out was pretty darned powerful in its own right. However, it could upgrade to Assassin and even the prestige class Grave Blade.

The other guide had been for another familiar class: Scavenger. Max had used Scavenger before, just after he'd arrived in this world when it had been a life saver, literally. Since then he hadn't spent much time in the woods and it hadn't even occurred to him to go back to it, until today.

"Well? Is it working?"

Max looked around. As before, he could feel the little heartbeats throbbing in the distance, calling him. They were just as faint as they had been last time, though that made sense, he hadn't gotten many skill levels in Scavenger. He hadn't really known how to power level his skills back then. The guide had said the ability became stronger as he leveled Scavenger, but that wasn't even the coolest part.

Apparently, Scavenger was a sleeper class. It was all about building health at the beginning, with mostly support abilities that weren't terribly good in combat, but when you got the class upgrade... Oh boy. The guide had called it: The Defiler and it was a class entirely built around retaliation moves and nasty debuffs that stacked over time.

If he'd known that earlier he might have stuck it out as a Scavenger.

“Yeah,” he said, turning back at a thumping noise behind him. It was Scruff, using all his tentacles to churn down the ramp as fast as he could.

“Scruff!” Max said. “I said stay in the ship!”

The dungeon crawler, now somewhere between the size of a small and medium dog was holding up four of his tentacles like a child, asking to be picked up.

Max sighed. “Fine.” He'd always had a soft spot for animals. He leaned over and extended an arm. Scruff quickly grasped his arm bones and climbed up to Max's right shoulder where the creature sat like a second head with medusa hair. The creature was now too big to crawl inside Max's chest cavity but he didn't seem to mind.

“I hope this works,” Trina said, turning back toward the dense pine forest nearby. “We really need some herbs. I want some Pussblotter, Fellenleaf, Moonshift and Blackbell... Oh and Stingweed.”

Just hearing the names made some of the pulsing beats in the distance quicken a little. It was exactly like the guide had said. The Scavenger's Rummage ability could sense what he was looking for. If it was near enough, it would take him right to it. Not only that but the chance of finding additional items of value was always higher as long as at least one person in the party was a Scavenger.

It was too bad they were garbage in combat. He remembered that from the game though. First Fantasy had a similar class called Searcher. You made someone one of those only when you really needed a rare drop. In this case, it was to get Trina whatever crap she needed for her bombs and potions.

"You're sure we need to stop for this?" he asked as he stepped into the woods.

Trina turned around. Her plague doctor mask had been left behind in the ship so he could clearly see her frowning at him. "Of course I'm sure!" she said. "Crafting potions and bombs that cause status effects is one of the most important things I do. If I don't have anything to make them with, my combat effectiveness is nil."

"You've still got your leeches though, don't you?" he asked.

Trina patted the pouch at her waist. "I do, but they won't help you, you dolt. You don't have any blood."

Max nodded. Right.

Despite it being late afternoon, the woods here were especially dark and filled with tall needly looking trees. They looked a little like evergreens from back home except they were rounded at the top and had thorns, big ones. It made sense though, they'd parked the airship on the slope of a mountain. Somehow Tela had found them a clearing with enough flat space for a landing.

It wasn't too far to the first thumping heart thing. He brushed aside a thick dark leaved bush to reveal a pair of very light colored plants, almost silver.

"Ha! Moonshift, excellent!" Trina said as she snapped the plants off at the base and jammed them into a burlap bag she'd liberated from the airship's storage room.

Above, in the trees, Max thought he heard something. He looked up, scanning the branches. Twilight was almost upon them and his eyes were starting to really do their thing, yet in the boughs above, he saw nothing but thousands of branches intertwined.

Max looked to Scruff. The creature was currently twisting and untwisting two of his tentacles, seemingly happy enough. It must have been nothing.

This all made him wish he'd stuck with Breeder. The enhanced senses had been handy. Without them, he felt dulled. Though the same could be said for Dark Mage. The speed of thought and the number of tracks that could run in his mind in parallel had been amazing, if sometimes a little too intense.

"Is there anything in these woods?" he asked her.

"That's a nebulous question," Trina replied. "I assume you mean things that would attack us."

"Correct, I'm not concerned about a hidden convention of hippy teddy bears."

She frowned again. "Just don't go eating shamtree fruit and you'll be fine."

Was that a veiled attack on Raeg?

"Don't make fun of Raeg," Max said. "He might not have been a genius, but he saved my boney ass more than once... and... he was my friend."

She sighed. "Can we continue looking please? I don't want to be out here all day."

"Ah ha!" Max said, pointing at her. "So there *is* something dangerous in these woods."

"Of course there is!" she snapped. "It's the woods on the slopes of the Valcas Mountains, one of the last wild places in all of Fohra! What did you think would be in here? A Slinkitty? Biddies to come and give you cuddles?"

Max tilted his head. "What the hell are those?"

Trina's lips pressed together into a grimace, annoyed that her attempt to heckle him had fallen flat due to Max's ignorance. "Just get going."

"I CAN'T BELIEVE how much we've found," Trina said as she pulled out a fourth sack, handing it to Max who already had three slung over his left shoulder while Scruff was still clinging to his right.

"I guess not a lot of people come up here," Max said as he noticed yet another broken branch hanging from a piece of underbrush. He'd seen broken branches all over the place, some even up in the trees. Something was moving around in these woods, probably many somethings. "Is this the last bag to fill?"

"Yes," Trina said. "Where did you say it was?"

Max used the index finger of his only free hand to point over to a clump of trees with very light colored bark. They would be almost white if there wasn't a kind of orange undertone. It kind of reminded him of popsicle sticks. "Feels like in the middle of those trees."

"Hmmph," Trina said, chopping at the spindly branches. They'd grown so close that the lower branches were almost woven together. "They're too thick."

As Trina hacked away, Max turned around, taking in the forest behind them. He could no longer see the ship down the slope, but that wasn't hugely surprising. They'd been following the little heartbeats further and further into the woods. Now everything looked the same no matter which direction he looked. If it wasn't for the slope of the hillside, it would be completely identical. It was a good thing he'd thought to mark some of the trunks as they went, because without that, if he got turned around in here, he'd be screwed.

"So we're going to process some of these herbs for us and... you said sell the rest, right?" Max asked.

Trina was puffing. "Yeah... I'll make salves and other useful potions. It'll get the gol back up. I hate having so little."

"Will they buy them?" Max asked, turning around again.

“Sure. I can make some that any shop will buy, but most frontier towns have a dark shop or two. I'm sure we'll find it. Melnax taught me a few things,” she said.

“But this is Reylos right? I haven't exactly heard great things about this place.” Understatement of the year.

Trina waved a hand dismissively. “That town down the hill is barely in that country. Father always loved to talk about how the farther a town was from their capitol, the fewer laws were followed. Of course, he always said it derisively. But for us, it's good. It means as long as we can get you to look like you're alive, we shouldn't have any trouble stocking up for the trip over the ocean.”

The trip to get Arinna. Finally, after all this time. Would she be happy to see him? Would she even remember who he was? It had only been a couple weeks but their meeting had been short, just moments.

In his mind's eye he could still see her though. The burns. The chains. Despite it all, that fire in her eyes that made her seem... indomitable.

“What?”

Max snapped out of it. “Huh?”

“Is there a problem? You started staring off at that tree,” she asked.

“Uh... No,” he said. “Well... Yes.”

Trina frowned and hacked at the branches with her knife some more. “Can't you help with this?”

Oddly, there wasn't a single weapon in their inventory that he could use as a Scavenger. Not even his good old spiked club but that wouldn't be much use against branches. He'd had that staff for a while, but the eagle had smashed it.

Max really ought to look into a replacement. If he was going to be changing classes a lot, it was a good idea to keep some equipment for each, certainly the ones he used a lot. This was the third time he'd been a Scavenger due to the useful ability and it probably wouldn't be the last either.

None of that was the biggest problem with Trina's request. "Actually no... I'm currently Scavenger level two. My strength is zero."

Trina shook her head. "Figures," she said and chopped at the branches some more. "So... what's the problem?"

"What problem?" Max asked.

Trina rolled her eyes. "What you were thinking about before!"

"Oh..." Max looked down at his black leather boots. "Uh... It's Arinna. What if... What if she doesn't..." he sighed. He rarely had trouble finding words, even if they weren't the right ones, something always came out when he opened his mouth. But this time, nothing was there.

"What? She won't want you to free her? Are you an idiot? Of course she will. I don't think that's the problem though."

Max looked up at her. "What do you mean?"

"I think you're worried she won't like you," Trina said. "I also think you still imagine you're betrothed to her. I don't care what your status screen says, you need to let that go," she added, pointing her knife in his direction. "If by some grace of Gazric we happen to find and free his daughter and don't die in the process... we should be happy with that."

But... he really liked her. The idea of the betrothal... was kind of cool. Assuming she actually was a human woman and not some undead horror. Not that he could talk, he thought, looking down at his own skeletal hands.

"Relationships are a waste of time anyway. Take it from me," Trina said. "Men are boobs, I gave up on them years ago. It's better to focus on your work. If you find some cute little bag of bones you want to... I don't know... make little skeletons with..."

"Just stop," Max said.

Trina laughed. "The point is... who cares if she doesn't like you? If we survive this you'll have done what you're supposed to right?"

Max nodded. "Yeah."

"Ok then," she replied, then frowned. "Oh... that's weird."

"What?"

"That necklace of yours. The eye is open."

Max looked down. "Really?"

It was. The eye was wide open, like he'd never seen it before. This was the dark seeking amulet right? It had opened when Trina arrived but seemed to have forgotten about her since. Had it decided to notice her again? Why would it do that?

Then there was a loud cracking sound from the brush behind Trina. It took a few seconds for Max to realize that it was the sound of tree branches snapping like twigs.

Scruff hissed.

Then he saw it. A massive scaly head the size of a small car rose from the brush, breaking branches as it ascended above them. Teeth the size of a man's arm ringed a long pointed snout.

"Oh shit," Max said. "That's..."

"A dragon!" Trina said. "Run!"

2

A LITTLE PROBLEM AND BIG BABY

Brittney raised her torch casting its golden glow across the bottom of the chasm. The floor here was covered in bones that crunched beneath her feet as she stepped down from the ledge. At the edge of the light she caught a glimpse of the frozen form of a woman, which she approached, passing several other bodies. These people had recently died but had already been picked clean by whatever creatures frequented this dark stinking pit.

She walked around the figure, squatting beside her to get a better look. The woman's mouth was open. She'd been caught in the middle of a scream as she'd turned to stone.

"Tsk tsk," Brittney said, shaking her head as she pulled a small vial from her inventory, pausing before removing the stopper. "Do I have to? These are expensive."

"Yes," said a voice from nowhere.

She frowned. "I hate rewarding failure."

"I saw what happened from the Oculum. It couldn't have been helped," the voice added. "There was... outside interference."

Brittney raised an eyebrow as she poured the contents of the vial over the stone statue. "Really? From whom?"

"Someone who should mind his own business," the voice replied.

Unfortunately nothing was happening to the stone statue. The liquid she'd poured over it was dripping down along the curves of the woman's face like tears, but that was it.

"Ugh, Kinnus sold me a fake softening potion!" she snapped. "I'll have that rat bastard skinned alive!"

Sometimes it felt like everyone she met in this stupid fantasy world was trying to cheat her somehow. At least that part wasn't unlike the movies. And there were no shortage of handsome princes, though most of them were too afraid of her to make a move. That was alright though, she liked that they feared her.

"I suppose I'll have to handle it myself," she said as she opened her class selection menu and chose Light Wizard. A burst of white smoke surrounded her. When it dissipated her clothing had changed to the white robes and hat she'd purchased in Mirathil three hundred years back.

Brittney took a moment to admire how it hugged her form perfectly, and the hat was cute too. It made her wish she had a mirror.

"You're wasting time. We have things to do," the voice said impatiently.

"Oh shut up," she replied. "That's what I hate about this place! A girl can't just enjoy herself. Somebody's always in my face. Ucara!" she said, pointing at the stone figure.

A white light enveloped the statue, casting a brilliant glow over the entire chasm. In the distance things with many legs scattered, startled by the light.

"Being sikari comes with responsibilities," the voice said. "I never hid that from you. I made it quite clea-"

Brittney waved her hand dismissively. "Yeah, yeah," she replied, grumbling. Did she though? From what Brittney remembered, the contract had been pretty vague regarding responsibilities.

Only seconds passed before the stone melted away leaving a woman, still clad in her armor. She gasped for breath, squinting and using a hand to block the orange light of Brittney's torch.

"What.... what happened?" the captain asked, still shielding her eyes. "A Wizard? Who are you?"

Brittney ignored the Kestrian, turning to address the empty air beside her. "Tell me who interfered. You know I don't like it when you hide things from me," she said.

"I'm not at liberty to discuss it. Suffice it to say... There are some who believe we are not trusted to deal with the skeleton."

Brit laughed bitterly as she put a foot on top of a skull nearby. It took only the tiniest pressure, just a fraction of her power to crush it to powder beneath her boot. "We who? The light? Or me?"

"Both," came the reply.

"They must not know me very well," Brittney replied as she crunched an old bone beneath her boot. "When I put my mind to something. I make it happen."

"It's hard to say. I've only seen them interfere once before and that did not go over well," said the voice. "I get the feeling he's a plaything to them."

"Who... who is that?" the captain asked. "Who are you talking to?"

Brittney took her hand. "It's me, captain," she said. "Beylara."

The captain's eyes widened, taking in her surroundings, feeling the bones beneath her. "You're a mage? I thought-"

"I'm whatever I want to be," Brittney said. "Now get up. I hate this place."

"What happened... I remember so little," the captain said, struggling to one knee.

"You should feel lucky," Brittney told her, grasping the woman's hand and pulling her to her feet. "You were the only survivor. I only came here because Cerathia told me to."

"The... the goddess?" the captain said. "You truly hear her?"

"I do," Brittney replied. "Am I not Sikari? Chosen by the goddess? Filled by her power? Blessed with the divine ability to change class to suit her will?"

The captain nodded, her eyes downward. Brittney knew it was partly because she was still recovering from being stone for nearly a day, and partly because few believed in the stories of Sikari, especially the rich. They didn't believe in any nobility but their own.

It reminded Brittney of her father.

She hated her father.

"Now get up. I'm not going to carry you out of here and there's some hiking to do. An airship from Kestria has already arrived. It will return you to-"

"No!" the captain said, gasping at Brittney's arm with trembling fingers. "The skeleton killed my hounds and took my spear. I can't go back to Kestria while he yet lives. I'll be disowned... The shame!"

"Don't touch me," Brittney said flatly as she peeled the fingers from her arm. She turned on her heel to ascend the path that led out of the chasm.

"Please... I must-"

"No," Brittney replied, continuing on. "You'll only slow me down. You can't be more than what... level forty?"

"Forty-three," the captain replied. "With a skill of-"

"Doesn't matter," Brittney said with a sneer. "I hit level ninety-nine before you were even born."

Max tried to run. He dropped the bags of herbs and mushrooms and bark and all the other crap Trina had made him toss in there over the past several hours, summoned his trusty spiked club into his right hand, and turned to make a break for it.

Sadly, the level two Scavenger, like most of the classes when he had them, sported a pathetic zero agility. He didn't get to take two steps before a clawed foot the size of a garbage can slammed down from above.

486 damage received.

That's what his arm display said, about a half second before everything went black.

When Max snapped back to consciousness the familiar pain of reanimation burned through his bones. The first thing he noticed was that it was now night. Hanging overhead was a sky full of stars shining like millions of tiny jewels sewn into a deep blue tapestry. He could see obscuring clouds of dark gas and dust in a great curve over head. It was like one of those photographs of the night sky taken far from civilization, which was certainly the truth here.

As the pain began to recede he looked down, checking his skeletal body. He had both arms, his ribs were fine...

“Crap,” he said.

His right leg was missing. The femur had been broken in half about a third of the way down and everything below that point was just gone.

“I guess that's what happens when you meet a dragon in the woods,” he said.

Still... it wasn't the worst experience he'd had here. He'd met a lot of weird fantasy creatures with funky names. Seeing a regular-ass dragon was oddly comforting.

The thing had been cool looking too, with dark red tinted scales and a particularly vicious aggressive mouth full of recurved prey snaring teeth. He hadn't gotten a good enough look at it to know if it had horns, or even wings, which was too bad.

He looked around. Nothing nearby appeared to be charred. Had it eaten Trina? She wasn't anywhere around. Nor was there any sign of the dragon. If she was receiving damage his display would have notified him.

He propped himself up on his elbows, looking down at the remains of his right leg.

“Guess my new name is Peg leg Knight.”

Movement from his right drew his gaze as something dark flopped out from behind a tree.

“Scruff! Buddy... I'm glad you're Ok! Where's Trina?”

He couldn't hear Scruff's thoughts. The little creature wasn't bound with a cattan like Mytten so while he wasn't one of the summoning classes like Breeder, he'd be forced to figure out another way to understand him. As it turned out that wasn't really a problem. Scruff didn't have terribly complex thoughts.

The crawler stuck out a tentacle to his right.

"She's down there?"

Scruff nodded.

"Is the dragon down there?"

Scruff nodded again.

"Damn," Max said. Of course it was.

He looked at Scruff. "Well... what do I do?"

The creature pointed his tentacle again, insistent.

Max sighed. "Easier said than done, my man."

He slumped to the side and dragged himself over to a tree. It wasn't like the usual peg leg situation where the pirate was tastefully missing only the bottom part of his leg just above the foot. Eighty percent of his leg was gone, that made things much harder.

Scruff pitched in to help though. The dungeon crawler climbed up the tree and wrapped Max with a couple tentacles to heave him up the trunk. The little creature hadn't just grown in size but strength as well.

The nearest stick big enough to use as a crutch was two tree trunks away, forcing Max to hop on one leg. He barely made it without falling. Luckily, the stick was just long enough to help him balance while he continued hopping from tree to tree. A look back showed Scruff churning his way through the brush. The creature didn't seem well made for getting around on land but that didn't matter because he was more than fast enough to keep up with Max and his super low agility...

Wait a second.

He shouldn't be able to jump around at all, not with zero agility, but he'd died! That meant all that Scavenging might have resulted in several skill levels. He paused at the nearest tree and brought up his status display.

Status

Boneknight Betrothed

Level	19	Scavenger Skill	12
Health	1/444		
Magic	1/1	Affinity	Dark
Skills Rekindle, Rummage		Magic Dead Weight, Teeth of Fate, Void Crush, Flame, Chill...	
Strength	0	Attacks x 0	0
Agility	2	Accuracy	71%
		Defense	8
Vitality	15	Evasion	1%
Mind	7	Magic Defense	5
		Magic Evasion	3%

Scavenger skill level twelve! With that last couple of levels after defeating the Kennel Master lady and her dogs, Max now had four-hundred and forty-four health. Good deal.

His stats had gone up too. Not a massive amount, but enough to get him above zero on almost everything. Agility was now up to two, which was why he could jump around on one leg. Strength was still zero though, that was probably the lowest attribute for a Scavenger, and magic points were still the same single point he'd had since the beginning as a Breeder and a Brawler, and a Thief.

Though, now that he thought about it, he didn't think that single magic point was from Breeder or Scavenger, he was pretty sure it came from the betrothed thing. Though why that was the case was a mystery. You couldn't do a hell of a lot with one magic point. Max missed Dark Mage, like a lot. So far, nothing had made him feel more powerful than that massive pool of magic. It had been perfect for frying enemies, extra crispy.

There was one obvious problem with running as a mage though: no Raeg. The big barbarian had been their shield. Sure, he was primarily a damage dealer, but that was more than enough to scare the hell out of their enemies and draw their attention. His mere presence had made it possible for Max and Trina to safely zap them and blow them up. Now Raeg was gone and they had no shield.

Max sighed. He missed Raeg.

Scruff pulled on his leg, causing Max to look down.

“What?”

The creature pointed a tentacle down the slope.

"I know... I was just checking my stats."

Scruff pointed again.

"Ok, ok."

There was a snarl from down the hill, followed by a roar. Scruff was right, the dragon was down there. Max shook his head, even as he quickened his hopping. Why was he heading toward it? What was he going to do with one leg? Swear at it? Call it a glorified lizard? If he had any luck, it would have a deathly fear of harsh language.

Though his luck hadn't exactly been great so far.

Max finally emerged from the trees into the relatively flat clearing dominated by the airship. Next to the airship was a fire and next to that was Trina, casting a black shadow against the massive chest of the dragon that towered over her.

"I said stop it!" she barked at the huge beast, waving her arms.

The dragon snarled at her again, baring rows of razor sharp sword-like teeth. Now that Max could see the whole thing, well most of it anyway, the sheer scale of it struck him. This monster was even bigger than he expected. It's body filled much of the rest of the clearing that wasn't occupied by the ship which it wrapped around before the tail disappeared into the trees on the far side. Actually, now that he was looking at it, Max was surprised the stupid amulet hadn't gone off earlier.

"You're not going to intimidate me, you big baby!" Trina yelled at the gigantic scaly creature. "Now give it back!"

"Trina! Are you insane?" Max yelled at her, while trying not to lose his grip on the small sapling he was using to steady himself.

She glanced back in his direction. "Oh, decided to join us did you? I was wondering how long you'd be dead. You've caused a lot of trouble for this poor guy."

"I caused?!" Max shouted. "It stepped on me!"

"He was just trying to get away," she said and turned back to the dragon whose enormous head was hovering just above her. It seemed to be eyeing Max with two big purple eyes. The pupils had been vertical slits when Max had seen them before but now that night had come they almost circular.

"Give it to me... Come on now," Trina said.

The dragon seemed to wince and turned its head away from her before extending a fore paw, which it held in front of Trina. The clawed hand was shaking and in the light of the fire, Max could see why: Max's leg was jabbed into the webbing between two of the clawed digits.

"Oh... ouch," Max said.

"Pleassse... be... gentle," said a deep rasping voice.

Trina reached out. "Don't worry," she said. "I'm just going to see-" Then, in a flash, she snatched the leg from the dragon's paw and tossed it in Max's direction before diving to the ground.

The dragon roared, flopping onto its side as it grasped at its hurting hand. The tail swung out of the dark and flailed around, clanging twice against the side of the ship.

"Hey!" Max yelled at it as he hopped toward his dismembered leg. "Careful with the ship!"

3

A BONE TO PICK AND A SHAKEDOWN

"Ooowwww!" the dragon whined in its low voice. "It huuuuurts!"

"I've got something for that," Trina said, her hands on her hips. "Stop rolling around and let me put it on you."

"No!" The dragon said. "It'll sting!"

"No it won't, it's just an herbal salve," Trina countered as she pulled a small tin from her satchel.

Max dropped to the ground next to his severed leg, pausing only to shake his head as Trina and the dragon argued. It seemed the creature wasn't planning to eat her, not that he could have done anything about it. That allowed him to focus on the task at hand: his leg.

It was no wonder the bone had stabbed so easily into the Dragon's flesh, the broken end was as thin as a needle. The top half of the femur was completely coated with thick black blood. Max did his best to wipe it off in the grass before he brought it up near his broken stump. If it worked like his jaw, then once he got close...

SNAP!

The bones jumped together like two opposing magnets. However, unlike his jawbone, which had returned to its rightful place without any trouble, this hurt like hell.

Max gasped from a searing pain as the bone fused back together. From the result he obviously hadn't gotten rid of all the dragon blood. There was a ragged black line that marked the division between the two parts of his femur. It was kind of cool looking actually, like a bone tattoo.

"I said come here!" Trina yelled.

What is going on?

Mytten had appeared from the back of the airship. The giant spider was still suffering from her injuries but was making an effort to clamber gingerly down the loading ramp. As soon as her eight eyes saw the dragon, she turned right around and went back inside.

I'm sure you'll be fine.

Max chuckled.

The dragon winced again, extending its hurting hand toward Trina who slathered the remedy on its scales. The creature startled when she touched it, slamming its tail against the side of the ship once more.

"It stings! Ow! Ow! Ow!" the dragon whined.

"Hey!" Max said as he tested his leg, before standing up. "Stop that!"

The dragon frowned at him. "Shut up skeleton! Or I'll burn you like a torch!"

Max laughed. "Go for it."

The dragon's eyes widened. "You... you *want* me to burn you alive?"

"Less talk, more fire," Max said. "Full on Kansas City barbecue. Give it to me."

"Max!" Trina said, rolling her eyes. "Stop toying with him."

The great serpent did a double take, looking at Trina twice before his eyes focused again on Max. "What are you?"

"What are *you*?" Max replied. "Some kind of big fat chicken?"

The dragon snarled.

Scruff was waving his arms, trying to get Max's attention while also backing away as fast as his tentacles would allow.

"Yeah, that's probably a good idea," Max said to his little friend, then he looked back up at the dragon. "Well?"

The dragon looked at Trina who was applying more salve to the affected area. "Are you boys done? Rik, why don't you tell me why you're so thin. Aren't you eating?"

Max walked in closer. "His name is Rik?"

The dragon scowled. "What of it?"

"Just kind of boring," Max said. "Also... Can I have a salve? I'm at one health."

"WHAT?" the dragon roared. "Just one! How can you be so-"

Trina held up a hand. "He's got rekindle. You can't kill him, so don't waste your time."

The anger drained from the dragon as his head lowered, inspecting Max more closely. "Really?! How fascinating! I've only heard stories." He used his huge flaring nostrils to take a deep long snuffle of Max's scent before turning his head and sneezing. "Ugh... he smells like any other undead: rotten."

Max shrugged, deciding to give up on Trina and call a salve from their inventory. He knew they didn't have many left, which was one of the reasons for the little foraging mission. "What can I say. I bathe in rotten slime."

Max rubbed the salve on himself, starting with his recently broken leg bone. Maybe he was imagining it, but it still kind of stung a little.

Health restored.

"Well?" Trina asked. "What are you doing so close to a town. I thought you dragons kept far away from people, especially light people. There's a town just down the slope."

The huge creature sighed, his eyes looked away. "I wish I could... It's... It's a long story."

Max folded his arms. "We're listening."

The dragon narrowed his eyes at Max. "Do I have to tell that... that thing?"

"Yes," Trina replied. "You do."

The dragon grumbled. "So be it. I flew here from the southeast. My mate and I had been living in the foothills of the small southern mountain range known as the Gilas for three decades, feasting on the local creatures, staying out of sight. It had been years since we'd seen anyone. Then, last year a group of foraging goblins came across us while we slept. Salkhi shot some fire at them to scare them off. They were goblins... creatures of the dark, she thought it unlikely they would speak of our location. I..." He trailed off, sniffling.

"Go on," Trina urged him, taking a seat of her own on the opposite side of the fire.

"I had doubts but I said nothing. We went on our way then, continuing the migration pattern we'd gotten used to... but... but when we returned the following year to the same place... there was an airship waiting for us and a Sun paladin. Salkhi... he... he killed her. He slashed my wing and burned me with holy fire from his blasted ship but I managed to escape."

His eyes lowered to the ground. "I still feel bad... I should have stayed. I should have killed him and avenged her death."

“Was this Sun paladin you met named Tesh D'al Pioshus?” Max asked.

The dragon's eyes flared in shock. “How! How do you know this?”

“You don't need to worry about him,” Max said. “He's done killing dragons, or anyone.”

Trina nodded. “He's a soul in a phylactery now. Imprisoned forever to think on his sadistic ways.”

“Yeah... I don't think he's going to suddenly see the light,” Max said.

Trina grinned from across the fire. “He's not going to see anything at all!”

“Oh ho!” Max said, laughing. “Good one!”

“The paladin is dead?!” Rik exclaimed. “Oh thank you! But... but how? You're... you're...”

“Just a skeleton,” Max said. “You're not gonna believe it, but I hear that a lot.”

“Rik, you must be the reason we didn't run into anything in the woods,” Trina said.

“Yes... I've eaten just about everything I could ambush or chase down. The rest have fled. I must move on or starve... but I don't move very quickly without my wings and I must be careful. If an airship spots me, I'm done for, it doesn't matter what country its from. They're all the same. They all hunt us.” The dragon looked away. “If I'm being honest... I'm so starved I've been considering going down to the town and..."

"Eating everyone?" Trina asked.

Rik nodded.

"What's wrong with your wings?" Max wondered.

Rik turned, extending his left wing. A huge gash was cut into the membrane turning what ought to be a thick, strong wing, into a set of loose ripped skin flaps.

Trina stood up immediately. "Oh I see. It healed, but not together. I can fix that for you."

"What?" Rik said, his eyes filled with hope, then he recoiled. "But... will it hurt?"

"We'll buy sleep powder in the town," Trina said. "I didn't find anything on this hill to make it, but I'm sure someone will have some. Then I'll put you to sleep and fix it. It's a simple surgery, not a problem at all. You won't be able to fly for at least a month though."

"Oh... Oh... I don't know how to thank you!" Rik said. "You've given me hope where I had so little."

"Well, there is something you could do for us," Max said.

Rik looked to him, raising a single scaled eyebrow. "What is it? Tell me."

"TELL ME RIK," Max said, leaning forward and meshing his skeletal fingers together. "Where do you keep your hoard?"

The dragon's eyes widened in surprise and something else: fear.

"I don't know what you mean," he replied, his eyes flicking to the side where they seemed to trace along the trees.

"Max, we don't need his money," Trina said.

Max held up a hand. "Where I come from, doctors are some of the highest paid people in the world. You're going to do reconstructive wing surgery on a multi-ton scaly beast. I'd say that's worth something."

"It'll save his life. That's payment enough," Trina said.

The dragon was looking back and forth between then. He seized this opportunity to butt in. "See skeleton? She doesn't want payment... which I cannot provide anyway. Because I have none."

"The name," Max said as he stood, gathering Scruff from the ground so the crawler could return to sitting on his shoulder, "is Boneknight, but you can call me Max. Now, stop fooling around and tell me where it is."

"I don't have any gold," the dragon said quickly.

"Oh, so it's gold?" Max replied. "Do you mean bars? Or what?"

The dragon frowned. "No! I mean... Yes. I have a little gold, or I did, long ago. But I don't have it with me."

Max laughed. "I don't have it with me," he said. "classic." If there was one thing he had experience with from working as a barista, it was cheap skates. They were all same.

"Do you have to antagonize him?" Trina asked.

Max stepped right up in front of the dragon's face, so that he could feel the creature's breath flowing over his bones. "I think you do have money on you. Probably a significant amount of gol, maybe even some actual gold bars as well."

The dragon sighed. "I do... have... some."

"Twenty thousand gol," Max said.

The dragon's eyes widened. "That's! That's preposterous! I won't pay it. Absolutely not."

"You will," Max said, pointing at Trina. "She deserves it. She's doing you a huge service that will save your life. Have some gratitude."

"Max..." Trina said, frustrated. "I'm sure he doesn-"

"Fine," the dragon said. He raised his uninjured foreleg and dropped two huge five-thousand gol sacks on the ground. "But you get half now, and the other half when the surgery is completed."

Trina's mouth dropped open.

Max took both bags and stored them in the party inventory. "A pleasure doing business with you."

Rik looked away, frowning.

"Think of it as an investment," Max said.

The dragon grimaced. “In what, a swindling skeleton?”

“In the future,” Max said.

The dragon only huffed in response, sending out a small puff of flame that turned a small dried out bush into a pile of ash in the matter of a few seconds.

Trina caught some sleep inside the ship after that while Max stayed outside on watch, staring at the stars, reading the guidebooks. From what he could tell Rogue might be a good choice for his next class. Not only did it bring impressive damage potential by focusing on many fast attacks with multiple weapons, but it had particularly high evasion as well which itself would function as a sort of armor.

The drawback was that the hit points were low, probably too low. It wouldn't help Trina to be able to hurt their enemies if the first couple hits put him down. He needed more combat staying power. The book listed two known class upgrades for Rogue: Assassin, which focused on stealth and critical damage to one-hit-kill but with even lower health, and Grave Blade which was a bit tougher with multiple stacking combo attacks and abilities that overpowered enemy defenses with the sheer number of attacks. Grave Blade could be awesome but he had no idea if he'd be able to unlock it. The guide didn't say how to unlock either of them.

There was always Gladiator. He could go back to that one maybe. It would certainly do enough damage and take enough hits. However, his impression from the trial was that it focused on one on one duels, which Max would rarely see, and wouldn't help him protect his party.

There was also the question of how he'd level Gladiator. What would he have to do? Kill people and brag about it? No thanks.

In the distance he could hear the dragon snoring. The creature had rumbled through the trees to return to the stand of pines it had been sleeping in earlier. Rik sounded like an old rusty chainsaw.

Thinking of the dragon reminded Max of the money. Twenty thousand, just like that. Actually... Now that he thought about it, he'd made a serious mistake. He was only now realizing it. Rik was definitely a cheapskate, but he'd parted with the twenty thousand easily, too easily. Max should have asked for more, a lot more.

"Oh well," he said, patting Scruff who was currently sleeping next to the fire. "Maybe he'll need dentistry later and we can soak him for more."

It was just after dawn when a yawning Trina reappeared, from the cargo door of the airship. She'd already changed clothes from her plague doctor outfit into something more like a noble girl's riding clothes.

"You ready?" she asked.

Max stood up. "I thought you were going to mix things to take and sell."

"Well now that you got us all that money we don't need to," she said. "I made a few items for us, but the rest we should hold on to for later. Here, take off that black leather and put these on."

Trina tossed him a folded pair of trousers and a tunic.

"Uh... these aren't going to keep people from noticing I'm a skeleton," he said.

She folded her arms, turning around so he could change. "Do you think me a simpleton?"

Max sighed. "Ok... whatever," he said and unequipped his armor, putting on the clothes.

"Are you done?"

"Yes," he replied.

She turned back. "The cloak too. Purple won't do, it'll attract too much attention."

Max brought up his screen again and removed the cape Vish had given him. "There. Happy?"

"Yes," she said. "Let's go."

Scruff hissed at him.

"Sorry bud," Max said. "You can't come on this trip. Stay with Mytten and watch the ship," Max said, pointing at the ship.

Scruff didn't look happy about it, his tentacles were writhing with frustration, but he complied.

They walked down hill until they came to an old game trail that ran parallel to the side of the mountain. They followed it around the side until they came to a stream. Trina remembered seeing a road that crossed that stream, or so she said, so they followed it down. Sure enough, they came to a small wooden bridge.

"Which way do we go?" he asked.

"Left," she replied. "Here, we're almost there, drink this," she said, handing him a familiar vial of aqua blue liquid.

"The human potion!" Max said.

"The ingredients we found were very strong. This might last all day, but I brought two more, just in case," she said.

"Oh," Max said, pouring the vial down through his jaw where it splashed against his neck and collar bones and soaked the front of his tunic. A pleasant warmth filled his bones, which quickly filled out with muscle, veins, organs and skin. Once again... he looked human.

When he looked up he found Trina looking at him.

"What?" he asked.

"Is that what you really look like?" she asked.

Reflexively he looked down at his hands. They were the same ones he'd had at home, right down to the little scar on his left pinky from that incident with the cat. He couldn't see his own face, not without a mirror, but he'd seen it in a puddle before and it had looked like him. Or he thought it had, that was a while ago though, back in Ceradram.

"I think so, why?" he asked.

"Huh," she said. "Well.. you aren't as ugly as I thought you might be. Not that I like you, that's not what I'm saying here. As I told you before. Relationships are-"

"A waste of time, right."

"Take off those rings. You won't need the bonuses and they're suspicious," she said. "Oh and hand me the dark seeker amulet."

Max frowned. Wow, that was weird to feel his face actually respond to a feeling. "Why?"

"Because you're going to be my servant and you wouldn't have anything like that, but I'm a well spoken lady from a good family."

"So I guess that means you would," he said, bringing up his equipment screen. "Anything else?"

"Yes," she said, looking down. "You have feet now. Do you have any boots other than those black ones?"

"Actually... I think I do still have a pair of old holey ones," he said.

"Perfect," Trina replied, striding away down the road. "Put them on and let's get going. I want to get back to the ship and do Rik's surgery before nightfall."

4

A BAD SIGN AND A RAT MAN

The overgrown trail they walked into town wasn't anything close to what Max would call a road. It consisted of a pair of ruts for carriage wheels, and not much else. Obviously it was not used very often. Brush grew into the path all along the way, and it wasn't long before they heard rustling all around them. There were things out in the weeds and bushes, and they were closing in around them.

"Come on," Trina said. "Let's jog this last bit to the gate. I don't want to fight anything."

Max needed every point of experience he could get, but he agreed. As a Scavenger he had no weapon save his own weak fists and using Trina's bombs this close to the town would probably get the wrong kind of attention.

"Sure," he said and jogged behind her. As soon as he saw the gate, though, he felt like turning around and running, full-speed, right back to the ship.

On one hand, this place was a lot like the frontier town he'd raided with Ciara in Lansalis, the one called Celain. It was surrounded by wooden walls with only a few dull-looking guards hanging out in front of the gate, all of this was very familiar. The major difference being that this one had the heads of orcs on poles to either side of the entrance. A dark bird-like creature the size of a crow sat atop one of them, using its beak to peck at one of the eyes. Max would have been sure it was a crow, if it wasn't for the short spiky lizard tail and the blotchy purple skin of its featherless head.

"What is that thing?" Max asked.

"It's a retch," Trina replied. "Now shush. I do the talking here."

Max rolled his eyes at her. Man, it felt so good to roll his eyes. "Sure," he said.

"And don't roll your eyes at me either. You're a servant. Act like one!"

The good news was that there weren't chains attached to floating islands hanging above this town. It was just some podunk burg on the frontier. If they kept to themselves, maybe they could get in and out and be on their way without any trouble. Hopefully.

The gate ahead was open, but as they approached the two guards stepped out from either side. One held a spear while the other wore a sword on his hip and a shield across his back. Both wore a sort of cloth tabard that was covered orange and white checkers. Mentally, Max marked them as The Creamsicle Boys.

"Who are you?" The soldier on the left asked. "And what business do you have entering our fair city from the south gate on the mountain side?"

"Right!" said the second Creamsicle Boy as he pointed his spear at them. "I bet they don't even have papers from the esteemed Kingdom of Reylos."

"Well... I..." Trina stammered.

Crap. They were screwed. How had these guys already figured them out?

The first guard looked at the second guard and then they both burst out laughing.

"Had ya there for a second!" the first guard said. "Didn't we?"

"It's no worry luv," the second guard said to Trina, wiping a tear from his eye. "We're just havin' a fun."

"Yeah... if we didn't let people trade no matter who they were, this town woulda' been gone decades ago, like dragons."

The spear wielding guard snorted. "Ha! Dragons!" he shook his head.

The guard with the sword held up a hand. "Of course we'll let you in, just don't go causing any trouble, alright?"

Max tilted his head. "Why would we-"

The guard shot him a look. “I don't mean you! By Cerathia's drawers if you aren't the softest young man I've ever seen. You couldn't cause trouble if you wanted to, except maybe for yourself.”

Trina stifled a chuckle with the back of her hand.

Max frowned. He was starting to really dislike these assholes.

“No, I meant her. This one's wily. I can tell,” the guard with the sword said. He winked at Trina. “I like wily.”

Trina's lips pressed together but she said nothing.

Max found his eyes drawn again to the dismembered heads. All orcs. Why? Had they done something? Or was it just because they were orcs?

“You like our handiwork?” the guard with the spear asked, with a low chuckle.

“No,” Max replied.

Trina glared at him.

“That,” the first guard said, pointing at the heads, “is what happens when undesirables come to our town with ill intent.”

“Or without, eh?” the spear toting guard said, elbowing his comrade.

They both laughed.

Max was having a hard time keeping his disgust from showing up on his face. Not all the orc heads were from male orcs or even adults. He thought of the refugees he'd met in the caves, how they'd helped him even though they were angry and afraid.

"Yes well.. we have business. Where can we find shops?" she asked, holding a palm out with a small bag of gol in it. Max guessed around twenty.

"Oh yeah? What kind of shops?" the guard asked.

"All kinds," Trina replied.

"How about instead of the customary bribe," the guard said as he took the small bag and dropped it into a small pouch at his waist. "This paltry amount is far too little... but if you meet with me this evening when we close the gate, say... six? Then I could overlook it."

"Sure," Trina said. "Should I meet you here?"

Max stared at her. Did he just hear that? Was she making a date with one of these scummy jerks?

The guard nodded. "Yeah... that's just fine."

"Good I'll see you then," Trina said. "Where can I find the—"

"The shops here are situated around the outside of town, near the walls. The ones you're lookin' for are to the right," the guard said. "And as I said, don't cause any trouble."

Trina smiled at him. "Me?" she asked innocently.

This almost made Max laugh, almost.

They turned right and walked along a relatively wide street that ran along the wall. All kinds of people, though mostly humans, were bustling around the streets buying and selling goods of every description. Max saw an armorer, a weapon-smith, even a stall selling some kind of saucy meat on a stick that smelled noxious. He was floored when Trina stopped and purchased two.

"Gross," Max said.

"What?" Trina replied, her mouth still full. "I was hungry! These are pretty good too."

The odor wafting from her was making him sick. He couldn't be sure if the stuff actually was terrible or if it just seemed that way because underneath the potion induced flesh, he was an undead.

"I told you to be quiet back there," she said, swallowing a mouthful of the stinky meat.

"They had the heads of orcs on stakes Trina," Max said. "There were children."

"I know!" she replied. "But we're not here to punish people for disgusting attitudes. We'd end up taking on every guard in the city."

Max folded his arms. "Maybe that's what they need."

"No... You said yourself that Ar... er... that *she* is our goal, right?" Trina asked, taking another bite."

Max looked down, nodding."Yeah, you're right. So you're planning to meet that guard?"

"Of course not," Trina replied, licking her fingers. "We'll be gone long before the time he said."

"I see," he said. So that guy was gonna get ghosted. So sad.

Trina was scanning along the line of stalls. "So... I'm not seeing any shops with the things we need." She cast her eyes back and forth, looking frustrated. "Do you have any ideas? I don't want to go from stall to stall asking too many questions."

"I thought you had this under control," Max remarked.

"I do," she said. "And when we meet other people, you can bet I'll do the talking, but I'm not sure..."

Max looked around too. Trina was right, the place looked pretty normal, just your basic market. Though the streets seemed more full with people shopping and talking and eating than they should be given the small size of the town.

His eyes returned to the armor and weapon shops. All the armor and weapons were basic-looking steel and iron stuff, but some of the stuff was lighter colored, almost white. Max suspected that meant they were weapons for the light. No black iron, or black leather and no dark cloaks. If they had any dark equipment, these merchants weren't advertising it.

Oh, right... he was a Scavenger still. Duh.

"Trina, what's something specific you're looking for?"

TRINA LOOKED AT HIM. "Empty potion bottles for one, and glass vials for explosive concoctions. Maybe a new robe or mask. Mine are old and worn."

"Right but what are those things made out of?" he asked. "I know the bottles are made of glass, what about the other stuff?"

"Oh I see what you're doing," she said, putting a finger to her chin. "I'd presume a better set of equipment would be made from spider silk, or reptilian leather. Oh... that reminds me. I got you something back in Ceradram and I completely forgot about it."

Max raised an eyebrow. "What?"

"We can't talk about it here, remind me when we're back at the ship," Trina replied.

"Sure," he said.

Spider silk. Reptilian leather. Max looked around the market. Nothing nearby... but maybe... maybe farther down.

"This way," he said. "Oh and you need sleep-"

"Hush!" Trina snapped, punching his arm. "That's not something we talk about."

"Ow... uh... Ok," he said.

"Think about it!" she said. "What could you do if you could put other people to sleep whenever you wanted?"

The answer was pretty much anything. Steal, escape from enemies, or worse. "I see your point," he said.

She leaned in and whispered "Sutnu seeds."

As soon as he heard the words, the feeling hit him and he followed it.

"Down here," he said. "Follow me."

Two stalls down. An innocuous place with a drab front. It actually looked like they were selling little paper dolls, but there weren't that many of them and they were pretty poorly made. Whatever this place sold, it probably wasn't dolls.

The merchant leaned in, his wide brimmed hat tilted just enough for Max to see that he wasn't human. He was a giant rat man with a long mustache. Rat people huh? This was the first time he'd seen that.

"What can I get for you kind folk?" the merchant asked. As weird as he looked, his speech was normal, probably better than Max's if he was being honest.

"I didn't know Musa lived here," Trina said. "I thought your people stayed in the west, on the coasts."

The rat man smiled, leaning forward. "Reylos has been cracking down on those it considers undesirables. So I moved inland until I found a place where I can do business in peace. For the time being, this is that place."

"Selling paper dolls," Max said.

"Among other things," the rat man said.

"Don't you worry you'll end up like those orcs we saw on the way in?" Max asked.

The rat man narrowed his eyes. "Watch your tongue. I'm no orc."

Apparently, Max had hit a nerve. Before he could dig into why, Trina stepped on his foot.

"Ow!" he said.

"Do you have Sutnu?" Trina asked the merchant, leaning in. "Preferably raw."

"Oh... no!" the merchant said. "I sell only paper dolls." However he then used a clawed finger to point to a small hand written sign on the table. On the sign was written: How much?

Trina frowned. "Oh... Well I suppose we're at the wrong place then. I'm sorry."

It was Max's turn. He jabbed a fist into Trina's shoulder.

"Hey!" she said. "What was-"

Max pointed at the counter.

"Oh," she said.

"As much as you will sell us," Max told the merchant.

Trina glared at him. "I said I'd do the talking."

"Hmmm..." the merchant said, his eyes darting from Trina to Max and back again. "Do you have money?"

"We do," Trina said extending her hand palm up but the merchant batted it away, making a chattering sound with his long front teeth.

"You two," he shook his head. "I would think you're Reylosian investigators were you not so inept. I have to be very careful. This thing you are asking for is... shall we say... a word we do not say openly. Do you understand?"

Trina nodded.

"I can sell you twenty cabits of the stuffing for dolls, is this acceptable?" The rat-man said, leaning back.

Max frowned. "How much is that?"

Trina's eyes flared at him, silently telling him yet again to shut up. She was right though, it was really stupid to give people the idea he was new to this world. Even if they didn't understand he came from Earth, they'd know something was weird about him and remember it.

"That's fine," Trina said. "How much?"

"Seven hundred gol," the merchant said languidly. When Trina immediately summoned the money and placed it in a good sized bag on the counter, his eyes widened. "Oh... If there's anything else you need, please, ask."

"Actually there is something," Trina said. "I need vials."

The merchant placed a small bag on the table, being sure to cover it with a ragged cloth so its contents could be seen by no one except for Trina. "You're a doctor?" he asked.

Trina leaned in and inspected the contents of the bag. Apparently the seeds were what she wanted because there was a poof of smoke as the bag disappeared into their inventory.

"Yes," Trina said.

"My name is Keenar," the rat man said. "There is someone who could benefit from your services. If you are willing."

"I could spare a few moments... is it serious?"

"It is my child. She's been ill for months," Keenar said, using a claw to pull on his thin mustache. "I thought she might get better once the weather dried, but that hasn't happened. If you help her, I can make sure you will never need for vials again."

Max looked around. "Why don't you go?" he said. "I'll shop around a bit. This place seems safe enough."

"Are you sure?" Trina asked.

He nodded. "Yeah... Uh... Keenar, where could a guy find, you know... some books, the dark kind."

"Ah... a mage?" the merchant asked.

"Sometimes," Max said.

"The armor shop, back that way," Keenar said, pointing a claw. "But be careful. I don't know the armorer very well. She is a recent arrival here."

Max shrugged, looking down at his clothes. "I don't imagine I'm much a target for robbery looking like this."

"So we'll meet back here then?" Trina asked. "Be sure to be back before the gate closes."

"Right... you don't want to end up accidentally keeping your promise to that great guy," Max noted with the edge of a smile.

Trina's eyes narrowed. "Right. And don't spend all my money either."

"Sure," Max said, turning around.

Her money, he thought with some bitterness as he walked back through the crowd. She wouldn't have any if he hadn't bargained with the dragon for it. Who knows how much more that scaly cheapskate was hiding. Maybe he even had rare items tucked under those shiny red scales. It was bad enough to be big and scary and make a guy look awesome if he could kill you, it was another to have a literal fortune on you. It was no wonder paladins hunted them.

It was too bad dark creatures didn't resurrect like the light did. Otherwise it might be worth it to go get a cache amulet for the dragon. Hmm. Actually it might be worth it for him. He had Trina in the party so the inventory wouldn't be lost unless they were wiped, but that wasn't impossible obviously. He should look into one.

Thinking about the dragon made him curious how Rik had gotten all that money. Earth's fairy tale stories weren't exactly clear on how dragons got their treasures, except for Tolkein's Smaug, the book said he stole it. If Max had to guess, the presumption in most tales was that dragons stole their hoards, but people often thought the same about the rich. It wasn't uncommon to lump together people who created a successful company with organized criminals. Maybe this place was different from the stories he knew. Maybe the big lizards here weren't thieves but shrewd investors.

That might be interesting to have a chat with Rik about, carefully.

5

A NEW SUIT AND SHORT TRIP

It wasn't long before he was standing in front of the armor shop. Behind the counter was a tall woman with long black hair tied up in a pony tail. There was a golden sash tied around her head like a thick bandanna. Her arms were impressively muscled too, which made sense given her job. When she saw him looking in her direction, she smiled at him.

Max was so surprised by it, he didn't even know what to do.

"Uh... hi..." he said.

"Here to buy something, or are you just going to stand there and stare?" she asked.

"Uh... the second one," he replied, finding his footing again. "I always try to make every interaction as uncomfortable as possible."

She laughed, smiling again. Man, it was so nice to have a normal interaction with a person.

"Are you in the market for armor?" she asked. "I make it all myself."

Max's eyebrows shot up. "Really? That's impressive. I'm pretty sure I couldn't even lift one of those hammers."

"I was an apprentice in Nikal, learned the trade from a master and set out on my own five years ago. Never looked back. What about you?" she asked leaning in.

Whoa... she was definitely getting friendly. That was unexpected. It was flattering though.

"Uh... I've been around. Here and there."

"Oh, tight lipped then," she said. "I'm Hallie."

"Huh, yeah. I... uh... I'm Max. I was told you might have something for me. Something darker."

She raised an eyebrow. "I see. You don't look like the brawler type, are you a mercenary?"

Mercenary, wasn't that one of his class choices?

"Uh... no. Is that common here?"

"Is it common?" She laughed. "You must not be from around here."

"I'm not... I've actually never met mercenary," he said.

"No? Well you won't wait long. They're more common in this town than black fleas."

“Why is that?” Max asked.

“The Reylosian kingdom is why. Here the royal family has a habit of picking fights with our neighbors or inciting a worker rebellion in the provinces, once a week or so. It's always something. So there's dirty work to be done for those willing to do it and it keeps me busy because mercenaries can use light armor as well as dark.”

“Really?”

She nodded. “They're tolerated by the light churches pretty well too. I think it's mostly because mercs just care about money and they don't ask questions. They do the job, no matter how dirty it is.”

“Ah... well that makes sense.”

“Funny thing is, the light has the same thing.”

Max tilted his head. “What?”

“Oh yeah,” she said. “It's called Freelancer but it's exactly the same. Same abilities, same experience bonus when you get paid for a job, and they can wear dark armor and use dark weapons.”

“No kidding,” Max said. “I guess they really are two sides of the same coin.”

“Absolutely,” she replied. “And I do pretty well selling to both of em.” she paused, putting a gloved hand to her chin. “I think I might know why you're here though.”

“Oh?”

"Follow me," Hallie said as she raised the counter cross piece allowing him to follow her into the back of the shop.

Max paused. Did he want to go back there? Was he being led to his death? She would probably be pretty surprised what happened if she tried to kill him, or maybe she wouldn't. Whatever. He'd already died so many times what did it even matter anymore?

"Come on," she called back over her shoulder. "I won't bite."

Max suddenly had a very strong flashback to years ago. It had to be at least a decade. He was sitting with his dad on the couch and they were watching a movie. He couldn't remember what movie it was but at a certain point a woman in the movie had said exactly that: "I won't bite." His dad had turned, looked Max in the eye and said: "That means the opposite of what she said."

He had the strong feeling that, this case, his dad was right.

"Well?" she said, putting a card on the front counter that said. "Closed."

Max sighed. "Sure," he said and followed.

The back of the shop was dark. It wasn't as dark as Vilnius's shop had been, but it was darker than outside. It was actually nice. Even though his eyes were currently human, the morning sun had been bright enough to keep him squinting. Finally the muscles around his eyes were able to relax. It was something he hadn't dealt with for weeks, something so small, but it felt good.

"You look out of place here," she said.

"I am," he replied. No sense lying. "Don't you have any help?" he asked, thinking about Vilnius's lizard... uh... person.

"No. It's just me. Can't afford anyone else," she said. "It's fine though. I'm very good at what I do."

"Which is what... exactly?" he asked.

"Armor. I specialize in the linked kinds. Mail, scale, ring, banded. You name it, I make it," she said. "It's exacting, time consuming work, but I love it, and it pays well."

"That's good," Max replied, not really knowing what else to say.

"Of course, I often receive things in trade. Things that no other merchants here will accept. I'm kind of a pushover like that," she said, leaning in close to him.

How old was she? She had to be at least thirty, if not older. Something about her smooth manner made him think she could be a lot older.

"So... no family?" he asked. "Uh... for you?"

"My husband ran off years ago. He was a Freelancer. I heard they buried his helmet because the rest of him was melted into sludge by a Dark Mage in the Minorin Dale."

Max paused. "Oh... yeah?"

"Which is what you are... isn't it?" she asked.

"No," he said. Not technically a lie.

She frowned.

"I wish I was though," he added. "Don't tell anyone but... I'm... uh... actually a Scavenger. I'm here trying to get some things, you know, for other people."

He could tell from her expression that she didn't believe him.

"Things like these?" she asked, opening a chest.

Inside were four spell tomes, all dark magic. Venom, Empower, Hasten, and Sleep. Max tried not to get too excited, but failed. Having a face with expressions kind of sucked sometimes.

"Ha!" she said, slamming the lid shut. "You are a Dark Mage! Admit it!"

Max looked at her. He needed those spells. Well, no. Actually need wasn't the right word. He wanted those spells. A lot. Especially sleep. Sure, Trina could make her powder but they had to buy those seeds, and it was expensive and dangerous. Magic on the other hand was an endlessly renewable resource.

Not to mention the traps he could make. Oh so many traps! Venom had to be poison, but how good was it? What did empower even do? Did it raise strength or modify something else? He really wanted to know.

"If I say I am... will you crush me with your amazing arms?" he asked, trying to be funny, but he was actually concerned she would do exactly that.

She laughed again, smiling at him.

Why was she smiling so much?

"Didn't you just say a mage killed your husband?"

"Yes," she said. "Should I be angry then?"

"Uh... I'd expect that, yeah."

"I should make you pay."

"Yes you should," Max agreed, though she wasn't getting angry at all, she was still smiling. It was starting to creep him out a little, "So... how much for all four of those books?"

She frowned. "I don't know if I want to sell them to you. Maybe we could come to an arrangement-" She put a hand on his chest.

"Look... I'm not what you think I am," Max said, taking a step back. "I also... " he looked up at the wall nearby where a full shirt of shining scale mail hung. "I want that too. It looks better than black iron. Does it come with a helmet?" He remembered having his jaw smashed off. "One with a face plate?"

Hallie's eyes narrowed. "Are you... even human?"

Max sighed. "Honestly, I'm not sure anymore. I... I won't stay like this... looking like myself, for very long." Trina would be really angry with him if she found out he'd told someone he was disguised. Probably best not to mention it to her. "So how much?"

“For the mail, with a helmet?”

Max nodded.

“Six-thousand five hundred.”

His eyes widened. “What?”

“I told you, my job pays well,” she said. “And you're right, it's far better than black or white iron. Dark steel is the next tier for dark armor and this is its equivalent: Sun steel. It has the same defense rating but like all the better light armors it resists dark magic, a little. The resistance can be improved but I'm still working on that part. If the price is too much for you, we could talk about-”

Max sighed, rubbing his face with his hand. “Fine.”

Hallie looked surprised. “Really? You have that much?”

“Yes,” Max said. “What about the books?”

“I'll throw in the books,” she said. “Nobody can buy them anyway. Dark Mages are hunted like nothing else. I'm sure you know.”

“I do,” he replied, remembering Melnax and Cheren. Maybe Trina was right. Once they freed Arina, they could set up a school somewhere and start training their own mages.

“You need all the help you can get,” Hallie said.

“You don't know the half of it,” he replied, “but thank you.”

"You're not really working for anyone else, are you?" she asked.

"No," he replied, handing her the money.

She gave him the armor and the books, which Max quickly stored. As much as he wanted to crack a spell book now, there was little point while he was still a Scavenger.

"Oh!" he asked, remembering. "Do you sell cache amulets?"

The woman paused. "Why do you ask?"

"Just wondering," he said.

"No," she said. "You'll only find those at a registered magic item shop, closest one is in the city of Rey on the coast."

Max nodded. "Alright, thanks."

"When you leave, be careful. There are dangerous people here and not just from the light. Steer clear of the inns," she suggested.

"Thanks for the warning. I will," he replied.

"Good bye, travel well," she said.

Max nodded, waving. "Yeah, I sure hope so."

Finally outside the shop Max wandered back toward where he'd left Trina. On the way he saw the stall with the little food on the stick. It still smelled terrible, like rancid rotting meat dipped in gooey slime. He kind of wanted to try one though, just to see what it would be like. He hadn't felt real food in his mouth in weeks. The closest he'd come to having real food here were those potions but Raeg had warned him away from them and for good reason too, from his own experience.

He missed Raeg. The last time he'd gone armor shopping had been in Ceradram. He'd bartered with Raeg's blood. In hindsight it hadn't been the nicest thing to do, especially considering the axe he'd paid for would now have no one to use it. It had been a complete waste.

"You gonna stand there or order something?" the vendor said. He was a short pudgy human with a balding head and very dirty apron.

"I guess... Why not?" Max asked. The sun here was still high, it was probably barely after noon. He had a lot of time to kill until Trina would be back around. What could it hurt to try it? "How much?"

"Special today: one gol for two sticks," the man said, grabbing two sticks and handing them over.

"Oh a deal huh?" Max replied, smiling. "How can I resist that?"

Max gave the man a single coin and took the sticks. They didn't look or smell any more appetizing up close. Maybe this had been a mistake? Oh well, he wasn't the kind of guy to do something half-way.

"Down the hatch," he said and took a big bite, wincing automatically.

It... actually wasn't that bad. How could something smell so nasty, but taste... pretty good? How was that even possible? Wasn't smell supposed to be like ninety-nine percent of taste? Was this because underneath it all he was an undead, and the rotten nature of whatever was on these sticks was actually good for him? It boggled the mind.

What was more amazing than the taste, though, was just the sensation of having something in his mouth, with cheeks to hold the food and a tongue to...

"Ow!" he said, biting his tongue. Dammit! He'd forgotten how to eat!

"Hey..."

Max looked back to the vendor. He was nodding to the side while gently pointing a thumb to Max's left.

"Uh... What?" Max replied as he bit another hunk of the slimy meat off the stick and turned his head in the indicated direction.

Hallie was standing out in front of her shop. Five guys were standing around her. It looked like they were talking. Some of those guys had clubs. Max felt anger rise. His first thought was that they were shaking her down, until he saw her point directly at him. All the thug's heads turned at once.

"Oh... shit," he said. He was still a Scavenger with no weapon!

"You oughta' run kid," the vendor said. "Good luck."

Max noticed an old broom leaning against the stall. If he took it and pulled the end off, would the wooden stick count as a staff? A staff had been the only weapon he'd been able to use as this stupid class. He might as well find out!

"Hey, can I buy that broom off you?" Max asked. "Two gol sound fair?"

"Uh... sure, kid," the vendor replied. "But anybody asks, you didn't get it from me."

"Deal."

Max snatched the broom, yanked the brush end off of it, and tossed a couple gold at the vendor as thanks. Then he bolted.

Acquired: Wooden staff. Damage 6, Durability 30/50, +3 defense.

"Woo!" Max shouted as he ran. It had worked!

His agility had gotten up to two after that last skill level, which helped him weave through the crowd. Even at this low level he was obviously faster than his would be pursuers. He probably would have gotten away if some kid didn't stick out a leg to trip him. Max smacked into two locals, knocking them both over before finally losing his balance and slamming into the ground with a long skid.

By the time he got up, he was surrounded. Five thugs, all humans, were setting up to pummel him with their clubs. Many of them were covered with tattoos and earrings. If Max wasn't on land in the center of a continent, he'd be sure he was being attacked by stereotypical pirates.

Covered in dirt with torn clothes, they were a pretty ratty looking crew. What were the odds they were higher than level two? Probably not high. Even with his stats as low as they were as a Scavenger, there was still a good chance he could beat all of them himself, but that wouldn't help him keep a low profile.

"Look guys... I don't want any trouble," Max said, planting his staff into the dirt of the street.

It was amazing how everyone around was just continuing on with their business, like someone wasn't being robbed right in front of them.

"Hand over the armor and all your money," said the man to Max's left, a big meat sack of a man. He was the only one without a club and probably what Hallie meant when she said: 'You don't look like a brawler.' This guy looked like all he'd ever done since he had the strength to ball his fists was punch people with them. "That's the only way you get no trouble."

"Alright," Max said, switch the staff to both hands. "But don't say I didn't warn you."

The leader laughed. "Get him boys!"

They all attacked at once, which sucked, because it was basically impossible to block them that way.

4 damage received.

5 damage received.

4 damage received.

Of course, with his health as high as it was, Max didn't really need to block. Instead, he swung his staff and whacked the guy to his right. The hit was solid, slamming into his enemy's right shoulder. The man yelped and backed away, holding his arm.

Max's new staff didn't do much damage, but these guys weren't very high level either. Max was level nineteen now with three-hundred plus health. They could come at him all day.

"Hit him again!" the leader said.

The three remaining clubs rained down from all sides.

5 damage received.

3 damage received.

5 damage received.

Max didn't even try to defend. He just stood there absorbing the blows. Now he kind of understood how

Tesh felt when he first ran into Max in the woods. These guys were a joke.

The big guy frowned. "I don't get it... Little guy like him. He should be cryin' for his mommy in the dirt!"

"My turn," Max said, lashing out with his staff with a two-handed swing to the left. The stroke smashed the club that tried to block it before landing directly in the center of the guy's forehead with a thok. The man yelped, falling to a knee and clutching at his head.

This was where, if these guys were light soldiers, Max would finish them off. They didn't seem to be though, and it was his understanding that the poor, dark or light, couldn't afford to be resurrected.

A crowd had begun to gather around them now. People were murmuring back and forth. Max couldn't tell if they were rooting for or against him. Probably the latter. He was the interloper here after all.

"I don't want to kill any of you, so back off, alright?"

The leader put up his fists. "Never!"

9 damage received.

7 damage received.

8 damage received.

"Oh! Three attacks," Max said. "Nice. But you're barely doing anything to me."

“You're not even wearing armor!” the leader shouted. “I can't believe you're more than level two... not with the way you look.”

Max sighed.

10 damage received.

9 damage received.

7 damage received.

Three more hits. They almost hurt.

Max retaliated by poking the staff out, aiming for the guy's thigh but the swing missed.

7 damage received.

8 damage received.

8 damage received.

“How are you not down!?!” the Brawler shouted angrily, spittle flying from his lips.

This time Max's wide swing hit the guy right in the center of his gut. The big man fell to one knee. Max follow this attack with another solid whack to the guy's back, knocking him down to all fours.

“I don't... understand it.”

“Sometimes it's better that way,” Max said as he turned around and left.

6

BURNED ALIVE AND LEFT FOR DEAD

The kid who tripped him was eyeing Max angrily from behind a fruit cart. With a striped bandanna wrapped around his head and torn baggy pants he looked like a smaller version of the others, like a pirate cabin boy. When Max passed, the kid lunged out and spit at his feet.

Max shook his head and kept on walking. The crowd parted for him as he past. The faces weren't filled with awe or admiration, but fear, not good. Max took the first turn into an alley and then the next turn into another alley, walking as quickly as he could.

After the fourth turn he stopped and ducked behind the corner of a building and peeked back to see if he was being followed. He didn't see anyone.

Finally, he slid down the wall and sat.

"What the hell?" he asked himself.

He looked like a person. He paid for things with money, he was nice and friendly, and still they tried to rob him. It looked like the shop owner had been in on it too. She'd probably called the thugs over and offered him to them for a cut, assuming they weren't already working for her.

Now that he thought about it, he probably shouldn't have beaten them like that. Now everyone knew he was strong. The next crowd that came looking would be bigger with better weapons and armor. Even at level thirteen he couldn't take that on, not by himself, not with a support class like Scavenger.

He should change to something else, but what?

"There he is!" someone yelled from across the street. It was an older woman in a long brown robe. This was followed by the sound of boots and clinking metal armor. Soldiers.

Wow, that hadn't taken long.

Max jumped up, looking for a way to escape. There was only one choice. He turned around and pushed his way through a display of rugs into the back of the store.

"Hey!" the owner yelled as Max barreled past him. The back wasn't a storage room for more rugs but a single room abode. A woman was inside, cooking over small hearth with two children seated nearby. All the heads turned to look at him. The woman screamed. The children screamed.

Max did the only thing he could think of. There wasn't any back door he could see, so he jumped out the window, smashing through a woven shade. He fell outside onto a pot filled with some kind of oil that shattered beneath him covering him in the slick yellow liquid. It smelled like olive oil but with cinnamon in it.

No sooner had he stood up than an arrow shot by, just missing his left eye by about an inch.

"Get him!" a familiar man's voice yelled. It was Creamsicle Boy number one, the one who'd hit on Trina. He was leading a contingent of about fifteen similarly attired guards.

Max scrambled to his feet and ran as fast as he could. The guards didn't suffer from stat penalties and didn't seem to be having trouble keeping up with him. In fact they were gaining. That did not bode well.

"Raeg, buddy, I really wish you were here," Max said as he ran, trying to see where the outer wall of the town was. If he could make it for that, maybe he could find a gate and force his way out.

Another arrow flew by, just above his right shoulder. The shots were uncomfortably close. Whoever was their archer was good.

Actually, with everything that was happening to him, what were the chances that Trina was fine and everything was going Ok? Probably poor. Well damn. What could he do? Go hunting for her?

"Come back here you thief!" the brazen guard called from behind him.

"Thief!" Max yelled back. "I bought these items fair and square!"

"He's a liar too! We'll catch him and put his head on a pole!" another voice yelled.

It seemed civil discussion was off the table.

Max turned to duck into another shop but an arrow speared through his left boot, sticking it to the ground enough to rip Max from his feet. He fell hard, rolling as his boot was ripped free. When he looked up there was an old woman standing over him with an oil lamp held aloft, her eyes wild with glee.

"Hey," he said. "Lady.... no... please no-"

The woman threw the lamp at him. It smashed, bathing him in flames. The fire caught on his oil soaked clothes, consuming them like a torch. There wasn't even time to get up.

Shit shit shit! What do I do, he thought.

But... it didn't really hurt. His flesh was charring and bubbling away.

27 damage received.

Just twenty-seven? Well... He might as well use this to his advantage.

Max stood up and raised his hands, reaching for the old woman. She screamed and scrambled to get away.

The soldiers had all frozen about ten feet back. They were staring at him, watching the flames consume Max's fake potion generated flesh, expecting him to die. What would happen if he just screamed and lay down? Would they continue attacking him?

9 damage received.

They'd probably expect him to drop something. Maybe a weapon and some money? Wouldn't they see his eyes though? Maybe not... it was noon and probably too bright out for the green to show up.

It was worth a try.

"Auughhh!!" Max screamed, then he twirled in a melodramatic circle and dropped to the ground. As he did he quickly tossed his burning staff and spawned five hundred gol. Then he lay still, skull down, and waited.

Item lost: Wooden staff.

Item lost: 500 gol.

"Huh," a voice said.

"Guess the old lady got him," another said.

"Where'd she go?"

"Ran off."

Max lay there, silent, immobile. Amazingly, it sounded like his ploy was working.

"By Cerathia I can't believe he just burnt up like that."

"Fool got himself in oil. Can't be helped."

"Ooh he dropped something. Oh... it's just that stupid staff."

"And some gol."

"Only five-hundred. They said he had way more."

"Better than nuthin'."

"I guess."

"What do we do with him now?"

"You're gonna give me that five-hundred, and carry his stinking corpse to the pit," that was Creamsicle Boy's voice giving the orders, Max recognized that sleaze immediately.

This was how, about twenty minutes later, Max found himself thrown into a massive open pit grave just outside of the town walls. His charred flesh was still steaming and smoking from being burned off his bones as he tumbled to a stop in the middle of the pit.

He lay there for a while, looking up at the sky, thinking.

Trina was still somewhere in that town, probably not doing that well. He should go find her and get her out of there.

He let out a long sigh.

He'd experienced a lot of stuff since he'd come to this world but this was the first time he'd been burned alive. Wasn't it? He wasn't sure. He'd died so many damned times it was all starting to run together. At least he hadn't lost the armor or books... had he?

Max spawned the book for Venom. It appeared in his blackened skeletal hand, like nothing had happened. That was good. So the only thing he'd lost was the clothes Trina had given him, that makeshift staff, and a few gol. No big deal.

Max stared off into the blue sky above.

Raeg was gone and Trina would be too if he didn't do something. He needed to pick a class and go back into that town and get her. The question was... which?

THE DARK WAS ENDLESS, flowing, moving, touching him, pushing him along. He didn't like it. He tried to fight. He wanted to smash it. Stop touching me, he thought. Stop it. I didn't say you could. You're not my friend. You're not...

There was a light ahead. Was this a tunnel? Hands kept pushing him.

"Alright!" he said. "I'm walkin'."

Was he though? Yes. He was. He could see his feet and his hands too. He was here. Wherever this place was.

"Don't you have any damned torches?" he bellowed into the dark.

No one replied. There wasn't even an echo, like you'd expect in a cave. It was as if his voice had been swallowed whole. It felt a little too close in here, like being smothered.

Then... Everything opened up and he wasn't alone. He was in a huge room with a great vaulted ceiling. Fog filled the room in every direction, making it hard to see.

He was in line, standing behind hundreds of others, no... thousands. There were humans and goblins and orcs, all lined up. No one was speaking. It was as if none of them could see the others.

"Where is this?" he asked the orc in front of him. "Hey!"

She didn't respond. He reached out and touched her shoulder. That made her turn toward him.

"Hey... do you kno-"

She turned back. Her dark eyes looked through him, seeing nothing.

"She can't hear you," a voice said. "I'm surprised you can see. You must be powerful."

He turned. The thing that spoke to him was massive, a towering creature with many limbs and slick black skin. Where a face might be was an unmoving white mask sloppily painted with smiling lips and eyes.

"Do you like my human face?" it asked.

"It's better than some I've seen," he replied.

"May I ask your name?"

"Yeah," he said, folding his arms. Normally such a creature might terrify him, things with many legs and arms usually did, but for some reason he felt at ease. Maybe it was the silly nature of the painted mask. "I'm Raeg."

"I am Kilthos a processor," the creature replied. "A pleasure." He seemed to be inching closer with every sentence.

"Where is this?" Raeg asked.

"This is the throat," Kilthos replied. "Where souls are sorted."

"Souls? So I died?"

"Correct," the creature replied. There was a mouth below the mask, completely separate from the voice. Now the mouth was open, exposing far too many human-like teeth. They glistened with a steaming clear fluid.

This thing was acting like it wanted to eat him. He turned to face it, frowning. "Come on," he said raising a hand and curling a single finger, beckoning the creature. "I dare you," he added through his teeth.

Kilthos lunged at him. Arms and legs surrounded Raeg as the mouth went wide. Any wider and it would eat him in a single bite. That's why Raeg dropped and brought his right fist straight up, smashing it into the creature's thin rubbery chin.

The blow stopped the beast in its tracks. The teeth cracked together with a noise that echoed enough that dozens of the others suddenly seemed startled and looked around.

Raeg didn't stop there though, he started pummeling the monster, mercilessly, slamming his fists into every section of the slimy black skin he could find. The creature was tougher than it looked but that was just fine. Raeg had begun every single day in the mines, with a string of crushing blows against the stone. It was one of his favorite ways to relieve stress. Over the years he'd worn the stone walls of his sleeping cell smooth. In comparison to that, this creature was like a rubbery slime.

Dozens of its hands came up, trying to get a grip on Raeg to hold him off or shield the blows, but the creature was too slow, and already dazed enough that his movements were fumbling. Fingers snatched at him, slapped him, and hands pushed, but without any strength. The battle was already over.

"I'm sorry! I'm sorry!" Kilthos cried, slumping down, lowering his tall form as he begged. "Please... have mercy."

"Why should I?" Raeg asked. "You were tryin' to eat me."

"You... You have power... I haven't tasted... not in some time... please," Kilthos replied, his many arms raised, palms open.

"Maybe I should eat you, huh?" Raeg said, leaning over the prostrate creature.

"No! No, please!" it said, quivering and trying to back away but Raeg stepped on one of its hands, pinning it in place. "Ow... No!" it shrieked.

"Tell me why I shouldn't, huh?" Raeg said, glowering at the creature writhing beneath him.

"I'll do anything you wish... I swear it, by the light of the moon."

"What are the words of somethin' like you worth? Nothing."

"I am bound... I am... I must abide by such an oath."

"Don't you lie to me," Raeg said. "Prove it."

"I... I don't..."

"Eat your own arm," Raeg said.

"No!" the monster shrieked, struggling even harder but at the same time one of his arms moved toward his mouth as if compelled by an unseen force. "Please! No!" Then he bit it, severing the black flesh above the elbow. Black ichor spurted from the flesh but instead of spraying against Raeg or the floor, it curled away like smoke. The mouth didn't even chew, it just swallowed. In less than a second, the dismembered arm was gone and the tongue was lolling out from the teeth, looking for more.

Raeg released the hand from under his foot and looked around again. The fog seemed to have cleared somewhat. Now he could see that there were many different lines and walking along each of them was at least one creature like the one cowering at his feet.

"Tell me, whatever you are. What is this line?"

"This is the line for the broken, those tainted by deep seated regret."

Raeg nodded. "Where does it go?"

"Nowhere," the creature replied.

"What's that mean?" Raeg said, frowning.

"It means... what I said. You may move forward, or back, but you will never get anywhere. You are stuck in the throat. Only souls free of regret, who've lived fully, may move on," the creature said, still groveling.

"You can get up," Raeg said. "So which line takes me to Divajin?"

"That land is closed to you," Kilthos replied.

Raeg grit his teeth, raising a balled fist. "Which... line?!"

"None!" Kilthos cried, cowering. "None of them! You cannot get there from here. I'm sorry."

"Why?" Raeg asked. "I heard my whole life that paradise awaits all after death. Dark or light. It's not supposed to matter!"

"That is... technically true. It does not matter the path as long as your life is lived fully," the creature gestured around them. "Look around you. Each line is for a different mortal failing. The one there is for those who lived their lives in hiding, never experiencing. And that one is for those who never loved another... and beyond that is for those who did so much they never bothered to live."

"So what happens to them... to us," Raeg asked. "We just wait forever?"

"Yes! Exactly... Unless you're eaten, of course," Kilthos said, his mask face angling downward shamefully. "It wasn't always this way... but that's how it is now."

Raeg sneered. "Gazric and that damned Scragger. I'll bet they had something to do with this."

The masked face tilted up and to the side slightly. "You would curse them both?"

"Damn right," Raeg replied. "If a land is all screwed up, you sure as hell blame the king and his worthless one-eyed servant."

"I... couldn't agree more!" Kilthos replied, rubbing four of his hands together. "In fact, if you truly feel this way, there's someone you ought to meet."

7

WRECKED AND RANKLED

Max stood up, brushing off his purple Dark Mage cloak as his black boots squished through the decaying organic matter he'd been thrown into. It was nice, he thought as he brought up his right hand and called a ball of flame into existence, that the sludge they'd thrown him into was thick enough to heal his health and his magic.

"They're such thoughtful people, these Reylos...ians?" he said. Even better, the headache was barely noticeable and his stats had been completely unaffected by the class change. Just like in First Fantasy: the more you leveled a class, the easier it was to switch to it. He was more than ready to rock and roll.

Max used his left hand to call the Shadow staff into his right hand. It was just after noon now, so Ruse would barely work, but it was better than nothing. He just wanted to lessen the number of arrows that found him while he went about nuking this god forsaken hell hole, starting with that woman's shop.

Interestingly, his bones were still charred black from the remnants of burned flesh. The color change didn't seem to be affecting him... and to be honest: it was kind of cool looking.

He walked straight for the nearest gate.

“What the hell is that?!” one of the guards, also wearing the obligatory Creamsicle uniform yelled.

“It's an unholy! Close the gate!” the other guard yelled, Just as Max unleashed a Bolt Lance that cut him in half. Both sides were cauterized by the discharge and fell to the ground, shaking with residual electricity. The Sentry next to him screamed and dropped his spear.

The gate was already closing.

“Oh? You think that's going to stop me?” Max asked as he used the staff to cast Ruse and stepped back into the shadow of a nearby tree for a little cover.

Heads were appearing above the wall.

“Where is he?” someone called. “I can't see.”

“He's there!” said another. “It looks like there's two of them!”

Max nodded to his Ruse generated doppelgänger and selected a section of wall right below the two voices. He had no idea what Void crush would do to a wall like this, but he wanted to find out.

It was a slightly better version of the palisade at that town he'd raided with Ciara and her goblins. Big heavy wooden timbers set in a line with cross braces, though this one had a second line of the timbers and some kind of stucco applied here and there to make it look smooth. Overall, it seemed pretty solid.

"Well not for long," he said and pumped seventy extra points of magic into a Void Crush that he directed into the center of the wall. He'd leveled up a few times since he last used this spell. It ought to be interesting.

It was.

The black orb hovered over Max's hand for a second while it absorbed the magic and then shot off to the point he'd willed for it, disappearing inside the wall's structure. There was about a second of lag before a perfect circle was ripped from the center of the wall and mashed into a solid ball of crushed wood pulp, plaster, and bloody body parts. This grotesque magical meatball hovered in the air for another few seconds before it dropped to the ground and smashed into a roughly circular pile of debris. Voices were screaming from the top of the wall as the rest of the weakened area above the hole collapsed.

Arrows started flying in from the left and right. Max decided to switch it up. The second level fire spell cost sixteen points to cast, not a problem given his current magic pool, and he hadn't tried it even once. Let's see... what was that called?

Right... Ball of flame, your basic fireball. From what he remembered when he'd read through the magic book, this one was designed for lobbing over obstructions. It worked like a mortar.

"Let's see, for arrow guy on the left... I'm going to say thirty three degrees," Max said as he stored his staff to summon the fire with both hands. The ball grew quickly. The next step was to look up and aim at the correct angle.

The fireball launched from his hands, arcing over the archer's position, just barely. Max then clenched his skeletal fingers into a fist and the ball exploded in midair, smashing a huge fiery hole into the top of the wall. The archer, now bathed in red fire, was launched into the air right into the center of the rotting corpse pile Max had just left.

"No muss, no fuss," he said, one second before an arrow hit his skull from the right with a clunk.

11 damage received.

If only these people were smart enough to rush him. They had more than enough people to take him down. His physical defense was poor, it was the obvious choice. Yet it seemed that as long as they stood, his enemies couldn't resist hiding behind their walls. Ciara had said something about that, how stupid walls were, how they just made it easier to concentrate fire.

Max launched a second fireball at the archer to his right. It looked like she was firing from a kind of watch tower. Not anymore.

The fireball hit the tower dead center and exploded, taking the archer and most of the tower along with it. Stone and shattered bits of timber rained down inside the town and more people screamed.

Max walked toward the gaping hole in the wall. Four soldiers with shields and spears had lined up there with three archers taking up positions behind them.

"Fire!" a man with a sword said and three arrows were loosed. One smacked into one of Max's left ribs. Another hit him in the right hip, while the third just harmlessly pierced his cloak.

7 damage received.

14 damage received.

"Boom," Max said, unleashing a third fireball. It detonated right in the center of the line, incinerating four of the soldiers instantly. The remainder lay on their backs, skin burned black, as they moaned.

"This is what happens when people piss me off," Max said as he stepped into the town. There were another dozen soldiers inside the wall but they broke and ran as soon as his green glowing eyes turned their way.

Defeated Reylos guards, Reylos archers, and Reylos guard captain.

You've gained a level of Dark Mage!

You've gained a level!

"Sweet!" Max said. He truly felt like a cartoon villain as he strode into the town with people fleeing before him. It was kind of awesome.

He held up a single skeletal hand which he clenched menacingly. "Now... you will bring me He-man!"

"Fire!" yelled another guard from behind him.

Max turned around just in time to receive an arrow in the eye socket.

21 damage received.

"Shit!"

He yanked the arrow out and burned it to ash with his basic flame spell, checking his right wrist.

80/240 MP

"We're good," he said as he slid to the right and looked down the street.

It was Creamsicle boy number one. He was trying to be a hero by leading three archers and two spear-men. Why did they keep hanging back and firing arrows? It made it so easy to...

"Charge!" yelled a voice behind him.

"Dammit!" Max said. Instead of turning around to face what he was sure was that group of swords and spears that had fled before, he ran forward as fast as he could, summoning basic flame spells in both hands.

Creamsicle boy's eyes widened. One of the archers turned and ran.

"Stop it! No! Hold your ground!" the guard yelled.

That's when Max let loose, throwing flame ball after flame ball ahead of him. He wasn't very accurate with the throws but that didn't matter when he was whipping two at a time. The baseball-sized fire balls were exploding all over the ground. One of them even hit a spear guy right in his chest, bathing his body with flame. That did it for the rest of them, they turned and ran, leaving Creamsicle boy number one all by his lonesome.

Max didn't care that he'd hit on Trina. It was none of his business who she dated and she was obviously from a wealthy family, so it made sense for a loser guardsman from a town in the middle of nowhere to try his luck. No... what pissed Max off was the guy's big shot attitude. There wasn't much worse than an arrogant dick.

"Stop right there!" the guard said, raising his sword. He knew if he could slow Max down those charging from behind would get close enough to join the battle.

"Not likely buddy," Max said. "Get out of my way."

"No!" the guard replied. "This is my town! Get out of it you... abomination!"

Max shrugged. “I see,” he said as he squatted and pressed his right palm into the dirt beneath him. “Khüchiig en bairluul, minii khüsel zorigoor barig.” he said and felt the magic power leave him as the spell was cast.

The man's eyes widened. “What did you do?”

Max laughed. “Wouldn't you like to know?” he said, stepping forward, walking right up to the outstretched blade before him. He could see the hope in the mans eyes rising as the sound of running boots and clinking armor closed in from behind.

“Go ahead, chop me,” Max said. “I dare you.” He kept walking, pushing the point of the sword back with the blackened ribs of his chest.

“Who are you?” the guard asked.

Max thought of one of his father's favorite movies. One his dad would quote, non-stop, all day long if he got started.

“No one of consequence,” he replied just as the leading enemy behind him stepped on the rune he'd placed in the road and a fireball exploded behind Max, wreathing him in flame as it immolated half a dozen guards in a fiery inferno.

The force of the blast blew Creamsicle boy right off his feet. He landed on his ass in the dirt, skidding to a stop eight feet away, his sword clattering across the street.

Max walked past him, unconcerned that the remaining guards behind him would try again. He'd made his point.

Now, where was that shop?

~

"JUST MAKE sure she takes it every morning and night for at least three weeks. Otherwise there'll be chance of fever and she's too weak for that. Understand?"

"Yes!" Fyena said, her clawed fingers gripping the tiny hand of her smallest child. "Thank you so much. We never imagined a doctor would come here. We'd planned to take her into Kylo. There is a healing temple of light there. We were told-"

"That they might treat musa if you paid enough?" Trina asked.

"Yes," Keenar said. "I've been saving."

"Unlikely," Trina said. "More likely, they want to keep your population in certain areas, like they do with the orcs."

Keenar's teeth chattered angrily. "We are not-"

"I know," Trina said. "But that doesn't matter to the humans here. To them you are all phohor, unwelcome and unwanted.

"But our origin is the same as the humans!" Fyena protested. "The same elven magic touched us both. They must know this!"

"They don't acknowledge it," Trina said. "You'd be better off in the south. You might check into Ceradram. It's a free city now."

"Free you say?" Keenar asked. "Free of laws? Of protection?"

"No," Trina said. "Free of the light. I saw the floating isles of Verian towed north with my own eyes."

"But... how?" Fyena asked as she brushed her sleeping daughter's hair.

Trina smiled. "I wonder that sometimes myself."

Keenar's teeth chattered again. "Once she has healed... I will look into it."

"Musa will be welcome there," Trina said. "All are welcome, certainly those skilled in the alchemical arts like yourself."

An explosion in the distance rocked the simple mud daub building they were in causing dust to fall from the rafters above.

"What was that?" Fyena asked.

Trina's lips pressed together. "It had better not be who I think it is." She looked to Keenar. "I have to go."

He handed her a satchel. "Here... as many vials and bottles as you could ever need. I fabricate them myself."

Trina was unsure until she glanced inside. It was a magic bag with an inventory extension like her own pouch. Inside were stacks and stacks of glass vials and bottles.

"Thank you," she said.

"That satchel belonged to my Aunt," Fyena said. "She was a Plague Doctor like you and helped many people before... before they killed her for it."

Trina nodded. "I'm sorry,"

"Don't be!" Fyena said. "I thank the gods for your coming."

"You worship them both? Gazric and Cerathia?"

Keenar put an arm around his wife's shoulder. "It's the old way... We prefer it."

"Even after all the light has done?" Trina asked.

"I don't believe the goddess would approve of what is done in her name," Fyena said. "Cerathia is kind and just. I worry... that something has happened to her much the same as the dark king, something terrible."

The idea seemed absurd but Trina wasn't about to contradict someone's religion. That was something Melnax had told her: if it doesn't interfere with treatment, it's none of your business.

Keenar looked worried. "Please... forgive my wife, she is-"

Trina waved a hand dismissively. "Don't worry. Your religion is not my concern. The health of your daughter is. Now, I must be going. I've got more shopping to do and hopefully not an idiot to save."

"Be well," Fyena said.

"You too," Trina said, patting the tiny sleeping rat girl on her head one last time before she left.

She arrived in the street just as a second explosion rocked the buildings. There were no airships above so that wasn't it. In the distance she could see a smoking wreck over by the east wall. Someone had blown the top off of a watch tower.

Max. It had better not be you, she thought as she ran toward the explosion. She hadn't even gotten a chance to look into buying new robes, which she desperately needed.

Trina ran down the street, taking a short left that would put her in line with the south wall where they entered the town. It was easy enough to do, the place was laid out like a pentagram, with walls on all sides except part of the north west wall where a short cliff dropped off to a river. If this commotion had been caused by Max then he could be returning to where they pledged to meet along the south wall... maybe.

Two of the orange and white town guards were fleeing past her, their weapons nowhere to be seen. Trina grabbed at the arm of one of them.

"What's happening?" she asked.

"Let go of me, girl!" the woman snarled, trying to pull away but Trina held her fast.

"Not until you tell me!" Trina said.

"There's an army attacking us. Dark mages and skeleton warriors have breached the wall from the south. You should flee while you still can," the woman said. "Now let go of my arm!"

Trina did, chuckling as she shook her head. "A dark army." If only it were true.

The two guards continued their escape, presumably heading for the north gate. The woman looked back at Trina with a scowl.

"Sounds like Max," she said, breaking into a jog.

It was difficult pushing through the fleeing crowds and it was a while before she finally caught sight of her skeletal companion in the distance. He was back wearing that purple cloak of his and standing in front of the armor shop they'd seen on the way in, tossing small balls of flame in front of the structure. It sounded like he might be yelling something too but she couldn't make out what it was.

"Hmmm," she said, mostly to herself. The street had been cleared of onlookers and there weren't any arrows being fired at him, so Max didn't appear to need her support at the moment.

Instead she took a hard left and slipped through a side street into the thin alley that ran behind the shops. There she saw a tall woman with very strong arms trying to drag a huge box out of the back of the armor shop.

"Where do you think you're going?" Trina asked.

The woman scowled at her. "I'm not afraid of some girl! Go away!"

Trina shook her head. "Oh no... No, no, no. You don't call me that. I'm not some girl," she replied coolly as she strode forward, taking a vial from her belt pouch. "My name is Trina Bill... and I've learned a few things about that skeleton out in front of your shop. It takes a lot to get him this angry. Tell me... what exactly did you do?"

8

POINTY EARS AND A NEW JOB

"Come out here! The next one goes inside!" Max said, which was a lie. He'd already blown huge holes in the town walls. With buildings packed this tightly together, setting one shop alight would take out half the town. He'd already been accused of that once and he didn't want a repeat.

Still nothing. She was probably already gone.

He sighed, looking left and right. That pirate-looking kid was peeking out from a clothing store two shops over. He reminded Max of Wyk... only dirtier and meaner looking.

"Well.. so much for that, I guess," he said.

"Ow....ow, ow!" a voice said. It was Hallie the armorer. She was being dragged out of her own store by Trina who was holding her by an ear. A very long ear.

"She's an elf?" Max asked.

"So it would seem," Trina replied, dragging the taller woman forward. "I thought she was a dark elf at first, under the influence of a potion to change her skin tone, but no, as insane as it seems, this is an actual elf. They aren't extinct after all."

"Elves are extinct?" Max asked, scratching his blackened skull through his Dark Mage hood.

Trina sighed. "Yes... er... No... It's a long story," she said as she dragged the elfin woman forward, out of the shop. The woman's thick muscular arms were hanging limply at her sides and she was dragging one foot.

"What did you do to her?" he asked.

"Partial paralysis," Trina said. "It'll wear off eventually. The lore about elves says they're naturally resistant to status effects. Even if I turned her to stone it would wear off in only a few hours."

"How long will that last then?" he asked.

"Not long," Trina replied.

"Stop pulling on my ear!" Hallie complained, fuming. "They're sensitive!"

"So what exactly happened?" Trina asked.

"Uh... I bought armor from her and a few dark magic books," he said. "Then she sent some thugs after me to steal it back, along with all our money."

The elf sneered. "You fool! They were supposed to kill you. I knew you were a Dark Mage! I...OW!"

Trina viciously yanked the elf's ear. "Be silent," she said to her, then she looked back to Max. "And?"

Max shrugged. "I beat the thugs but then the guards came and I had to run... it became a whole thing. They set me on fire, I played dead, now here we are. We should leave. This is wasting our time."

"Didn't you have something to say to her?" Trina asked. "You were threatening to burn her shop."

"Yeah... well I wouldn't really do that. I just wanted to know why she set me up. Now we know. She's a jerk."

Hallie spit at him. "You disgust me! Wearing the skin of a human doesn't make you one. You're just a grotesque mockery of a man!"

Max looked to Trina. "Charming, isn't she?"

Trina laughed and suddenly let go of the elf's ear. This caused Hallie to stumble and collapse into the dirt. She looked up at them, her teeth bared. "You'll be hunted down and destroyed. I promise you. The tyranny of the dark will never return!"

Max laughed. "From what I've seen tyranny is already here," he replied, "and the dark has nothing to do with it."

"What should we do with her?" Trina asked.

"We'll burn her alive," Max said.

Trina and Hallie's eyes widened.

"OR... maybe we'll leave this one... so she can tell her elf brothers and sisters I'm coming for them. You hear me? Tell the Keeblers and the Cobblers and that tall asshole who lives in Manhattan!"

"I... Alright," Trina replied.

It was an easy trot to the gate after that. Max only stopped to burn the stakes with the orc heads on them. It was the least he could do. He didn't know what they did, if anything, but nobody deserved that kind of treatment.

When they were about half way back to the ship Trina looked back at him. "So... I just wanted to say... uh... that I have some things."

"Oh right, you mentioned something you got for me in Ceradram."

Trina nodded. "Yes... that. I suppose we should start with that."

"Start?" Max asked.

Trina's eyes looked away. "I... I've been holding out on you."

"I know about the letters," he said.

"You saw them?"

"I saw that and a few other things, back in the school vault."

"Ah," she said. "Did you read them?"

"No," Max replied. "You're overestimating the amount of time I had there. Plus, I'm going to be honest... I was a little ticked off with you at the time."

"Yeah," she said, her eyes lowering. "Well... My pouch can store items like an inventory and it's not shared. It's a way to keep things to myself."

"I'm fine with it," Max said.

"Really?" Trina replied.

"Yeah... It's your stuff. We don't have to share everything. It's fine."

She nodded. "I appreciate that. I've been keeping this one thing though... and I'm pretty sure it's something you can use," she said pulling a large ring from her pouch.

"What is that?" Max asked.

"I'm honestly not sure. I can't use it and I don't even get an item description when I hold it. I think it's locked to a certain class or race."

"Was it his?" Max asked.

Trina nodded, staring at the ring. It had gems of all four dark affinities but at the center was a stone of pure black.

"You don't have to give it-"

She placed it in his hand. "Take it. Melnax would want that."

Acquired: Dusk Signet Ring.

"Whoa..." he said.

"What is it?" she asked, pausing to flip up her own display of their inventory. "Augh! It doesn't even show up for me!"

"It's interesting," Max said. "It says it's a dusk signet ring. Signet... aren't those for signing documents?"

"If you're a noble, yes," she said.

"It's listed like it's a key item. Usually those are things I can do something special with... but it also shows... Whoa!"

Trina's eyes widened with excitement. "What? Tell me!"

"Plus six to mind, plus six to vitality, plus six to strength," he said. Max tried to equip it, replacing one of his one point mind rings. It worked! "And I can use it!"

"How!? How is that possible?"

Max shrugged. "I'm just great."

Trina looked off in the distance. "I don't understand... Why you?"

"I don't know. Maybe it's specially made for someone who's doing this task, trying to free Arinna, or maybe it's just hard-locked to undead."

Trina's hand went to her chin. "Maybe."

"Look, I don't need these other three mind rings now," Max said. "They're yours."

"Really?" she replied as he placed the three rings in her gloved hand.

"Your class is mind heavy and a few extra points never hurt anyone. Besides, I'm probably going to have to switch away from Dark Mage. I love spells, but this team needs a shield and without Raeg, that's gonna have to be me."

Trina's eyes lowered again. "I'm sorry about Raeg," she said.

Max sighed. "I know. So, that was it? The ring?"

"Oh... uh, actually no," Trina reached into her pouch and brought out a long piece of vibrant violet cloth. It was incredible, shimmering but also shedding light, almost like it was drinking it in. He'd seen something like this before.

"The spiders made this," he said.

She handed it to him. "Yes," she said. "One of them mentioned you wanted one. I assume it's meant for Arinna. I don't know why you want a gift for a woman you don't even know, and a god at that, but I picked it up for you."

The scarf had almost no weight to it. It was gorgeous, exactly what he would have chosen. "Thank you," he said. "I... I really appreciate this."

"It's nothing," she said. "I hope she likes it and I'm glad the ring works for you."

Max stored the scarf for later and looked down at the ring. It said it was a signet ring but he hadn't seen anything engraved on it when Trina handed it over. He wondered...

"Ha!"

"What?" Trina asked, looking over.

"It's a little skull with rays of light coming out above and swirls below."

"Interesting," she said. "The sun burst is the symbol of light. It's also the seal for the house of Cerathia. But the tentacles, those surround the moon on the seal of house Gazric. So yours... is like a mix," she said. "Odd."

Max shrugged and walked on. "Whatever... Let's get back, sew up that dragon and get the hell out of here."

"Oh... No," Trina said softly but her tone was grave.

He looked at her, she was looking up the mountain in the direction of the ship. A single column of black smoke was rising from the forest up there.

Max broke into a run.

THAT UGLY BLACK creature was scuttling ahead down a tunnel that seemed to wind both up and down at the same time. There was a sort of wet mist that ran along the floor that was thicker than it should be. Every step Raeg took it would slosh and reform a little too quickly, like it wanted something from his feet. It made him shudder just thinking about it.

That was the other thing. His feet and hands weren't exactly solid either. They were see-through, like a dirty ale glass, and it looked like it was gettin' worse. He could barely see the tips of his fingers and toes anymore.

"Keep close," Kilthos said, swinging the masked top of his body around to face Raeg while the rest of him continued clambering ahead.

Raeg grunted in response. He was following but also looking for a chance to make a run for it. He didn't know where he wanted to get to, but it sure wasn't here.

Maybe that weird thing was telling the truth and he actually was dead, that was starting to feel more likely. He couldn't remember much before he showed up in that line, but there was something. It was more of a feeling, than a memory, a kind of hurt, but about someone else. Kind of like he'd let somebody down.

Regret. That multi-armed creep had said something like that.

Yeah, that was the feeling.

"Almost there." Kilthos said as they approached a series of orifice like holes in the floor and ceiling.

Raeg balked. "No... I'm not goin' in those."

Kilthos moved to the third one over, pointing into it with three of his hands. "You will. In only a few moments more you'll be weak enough that I'll be able to eat you."

Raeg sneered, balling his hands into fists. "You... You..."

"Don't waste your breath cursing me. Go down this hole, or I'll be forced to dispose of you myself," he said as a long thin tongue slid out of his mouth and rubbed along the outside of his lips.

Raeg felt himself gag.

“Ugh...” he said. He could feel it. His hands didn't want to stay up, they wanted to drop to his sides, to hang limp. He was feeling tired.

“Go or don't,” The masked horror said. “You have about four more seconds to decide.”

Raeg grumbled. He hated being forced to do anything, ever. He walked up to the indicated hole and jumped.

He fell and floated and spun. Every single second of it was terrible. Until finally, after what felt like forever, he slapped into a slimy, mucous-like muck.

When he tried to get up, he couldn't. His arms and legs wouldn't move.

Then something moved underneath him. He was sliding along the floor suspended on something that looked a lot like a wet slimy tongue.

“I hate this place,” he said as the thick muscular thing he was stuck to rolled up and suddenly flicked, throwing him across a great open space. Everything was spinning around him until he landed on his chest on the floor.

“Who... are you?” asked a deep voice.

At least it wasn't bugs, he told himself, as he dragged his body to his knees. He looked around for the source of the voice but saw no one. The room was dimly lit by a series of warm lanterns.

"Who's askin'?" he asked. His hands were barely visible now, almost nothing.

"Hmph," the voice said. "You have spirit. Most who arrive here cower and snivel like idiots. I hate that."

"Me too," Raeg agreed. "Nuthin' worse than a whiner."

"Indeed," said the deep voice as a form emerged from the shadows. Clawed hands, hoof-like feet, and a head of curled horns and jagged shark teeth.

"I guess you're a demon," Raeg said, fighting to stand.

"I heard... that you have little love for the dark king and those in his service," the demon said, stepping forward.

"Yeah," Raeg replied. "You heard right."

"Why is that?" the demon asked as it sat down in a chair that had appeared behind it.

"Gazric," Raeg said, almost spitting the name. "He's given up on the dark. He's given up on us. There's no other explanation for what's happening now. He fled like a coward and now we're all slaves when we're not outright murdered. I hope he never comes back. He doesn't deserve to rule anything."

The demon clapped slowly. "Well said, barbarian. Tell me, how do you feel about killing?"

"Love it," Raeg said.

"We have a great many here who've betrayed the dark, they need to be... dealt with."

Raeg grinned. "Sounds like fun."

"And finally... are you team player?"

"Absolutely not," Raeg replied.

The demon smiled. "Very well, I, Helran Malagus, fourth secretary of the pit, grant you a work permit, third class. We need souls like you. Now go do the dark proud."

A chain appeared around his neck with a little silver tag on it. Instantly, Raeg felt better. His hands and feet were solid again.

"Uh... thanks?" he said.

"Report to Vigolos on the tenth level," Malagus said. "Now... go!"

The instant the words were uttered, Raeg was utterly torn from existence. It was like a meat hook had ripped into his spine from behind and dragged him through a hole in reality.

The next thing he knew he was vomited out on what looked like a regular street in one of the worse parts of Ceradram. Actually no... it was more like Neman that crummy port city full of Musa... Or... Maybe it was like both of them, or none. It was kind of drab and ugly with a vague feeling like at any minute someone was gonna try to sell you something you didn't want to buy.

"Barbarian... This way," called a voice from an alley nearby. Two eyes shined from the dark there. The form around them was human-shaped but bent, like an old man. Raeg leaned in to see if he could see better. The guy hiding in the dark wore a long cloak with a hood that obscured his face. From inside the hood two eyes shined like the moon on a cloudless night.

"There you are!" said a smooth voice from the street ahead.

Raeg's head turned to see a thin dark elf striding down the street. He wore long flowing robes of black and red and his thumbs were hooked into his belt in a relaxed way. His expression was at ease, as was his hair which stuck out haphazardly from his head making it look like he'd just gotten up. The man could be out taking a stroll in an open-air market, not the underworld.

When Raeg glanced back at the alley, the eyes had gone.

"You're Raeg, right?" the elf asked, his black eyebrows raised and a smile on his lips.

"Yeah."

"See something over there?"

"Huh?"

The elf pointed with one thin finger in the direction of the alley.

"Uh, yeah. Somebody called to me."

"Get used to it," he replied. "Lots of trash in Narak, especially this part. Most of them are former employees who've been dismissed and gotten bitter about it. Can't be helped. You just have to avoid them."

"Oh..." Raeg said, scratching his head. Still bald. Oh well.

"I'm Vigolos. I'll be your superior. Come, I'll get you something to eat and we'll talk about your job."

"There's food here?"

"You bet there is," the dark elf said with a grin. "My treat."

9

GLOOMY AND MISERABLE

When they cleared the trees, the dragon was nowhere to be found. Instead there was a second airship, a lumpy, ratty looking one, parked right next to their own. A half dozen men were lying on the ground near the fire pit they'd left in the morning. The smoke wasn't coming from Max's airship but from the pirate's but Max wasn't sure why that was.

“What the hell happened here?” he asked.

Max? Have you returned?

It was Mytten. “Mytten? Where are you? Where's Scruff? What happened?”

I've been calling for you. You must have been too far. I gave up.

“Ask her where she is!” Trina said.

“I'm here now, outside the ship. Where are you?” Max asked.

We're in the flying room with the pegasus girl.

"They're on the bridge," he said. "Let's go."

"Wait," Trina said. "Here. Our last Salve."

Max frowned, holding her hand away. "No! Save it for the others."

"But your health and magic is down and it'll be close quarters in there."

Actually, she had a point. He brought up his status.

Status	Boneknight	Betrothed	
Level	20	Dark Mage Skill	37
Health	402/495		
Magic	34/240	Affinity	Dark
Skills Rekindle, Scan		Magic Dead Weight, Teeth of Fate, Void Crush, Flame, Chill...	
Strength	8	Attacks x 2	4
Agility	15	Accuracy	83%
		Defense	14
Vitality	26	Evasion	14%
Mind	41	Magic Defense	35
		Magic Evasion	17%

Trina was partially right, Max's health was fine, but his magic was low, way low, down to only thirty four points. The better spells would be more or less off the table. However, the real problem was that his magic wasn't well suited for use inside a ship. He'd blow the thing to hell and then how would they get to Arinna? The pirate ship looked like a flying garbage can, so there was no way he wanted to trade down to that. He had to do something though, and quickly. He could hear people yelling inside the ship and a hammering sound that was getting louder.

They're banging on the door. It won't last much longer.

"Ok... I have an idea," he said. He looked at Trina. "Back off a bit."

She did, taking several steps back.

Max summoned the sleep spell book into his hands. On the cover were several; ornate runes, half were written in Demonic and the other, he presumed were Angelic. He only knew the meaning of the demonic ones though 'Ayuultai noir': Dangerous slumber. He opened the book. As with Flame and all the others, the pages were empty. He waited only a half a second before the pulse of light poured fourth into his eye sockets.

Learned: Sleep.

"Now the dangerous part," he said, really glad he'd done all that practicing back at the cabin.

He thought: Sleep as he squatted and pressed his palm to the ground. "Khüchiig en bairluul," he said in High demonic.

Nothing happened.

He looked to Trina.

"What?" she asked, while he'd been using the book she had changed back into her Plague Doctor robes. "Did you ruin it?"

"No! I..." Did he? Had he missed something? "Maybe."

The thumping was getting louder in the ship as was the yelling. There was too much going on for him to think clearly!

Now would be a good time to come in here.

"I know Mytten!" Max said, as he stored the Sleep book and brought out the general magic book.

"Do you really have time to consult the book?!" Trina asked him.

"I don't know what else to do! I need to change my class but not have a massive stat penalty. I can't cast sleep on myself after I've changed my class unless I make a rune for it. How long will it take you to grind those seeds?"

"A long time," Trina said. "I'm going in."

"What?" Max said. "No!"

She didn't listen though, she was already going.

Well.. there was always plan B. He had a class where stats didn't matter as much. He quickly unequipped his Dark Mage equipment and switched to the selection screen, pressing Breeder.

His head swam for a few seconds but it wasn't actually that bad. Like Dark Mage he'd gotten to skill level twenty-seven in Breeder. That seemed high enough to mitigate most of the class change problems. There wasn't time to check his status, Trina was almost to the airship's cargo ramp.

"Wait!" he called to her, equipping his drain sword and the leather armor.

She turned back, her long nosed mask swinging around. "No! We can't!" she shouted and pulled a small vial from her waist. "This might help a bit," she said as she tossed the vial into the dark of the ship beyond. There was a sharp crack as the vial exploded and whatever was inside dispersed.

Seeing the vial in her hand reminded him of something though. Something that might be able to help. What was it? Ah! Yes!

He summoned a cattan to his hand. It had a symbol on it like a coiled serpent.

"Here goes nothing," he said. "Bind Gloom Asp."

Reggie added.

"Reggie?" Max said.

Shut up and leave me alone.

Welling up from the cattan, Max was treated to a deep sullen feeling. Was this a depressed snake? Definitely not what he was expecting from a reptile.

Max threw the cattan to the ground. A poof of purple smoke became a ten foot long coiled snake. It looked a lot like a cobra, only the frill was longer with a scalloped edge. The head swiveled in Max's direction and a long forked tongue flicked out.

You're a skeleton?

"Yeah... That's what it looks like. Come on, I need your help," Max said.

Do I have to? The snake's head lolled down. *I hate this kind of thing.*

"You hate fighting?" Max said, shaking his head. "I don't have time for this," he said. "The enemy's inside that ship, they're about to hurt my friends. Please," he added and ran for the ramp where a thick gray smoke was billowing from inside. Apparently it was the result of whatever Trina had tossed in.

Trina was already gone, having disappeared inside and Max ran in after her. The smoke was pretty thick but it wasn't enough to impede his vision, which seemed to cut though it well enough.

The airship, though a lot bigger than the little shuttle they'd had before, still only had one main corridor. It was a relatively thin hallway that went up and down along one side of the spine of the ship with bulkheads along the way. Max saw Trina hiding in a doorway ahead with what appeared to be eight enemies lined up against the door to the bridge. Several of them were holding a thick bar of metal that they were using to slam against the door.

"The ship's on fire!" said one of them.

"A big man in front turned around. No it isn't, something's been set off. Melk, Shaena, check if the owners have returned. They're probably trying to smoke us out, be careful."

"You're right about that," Max said as he jammed the point of his sword into the three nearest nearest ship thieves in quick succession.

13 health received.

11 health received.

9 health received.

Ahhh, that felt good. It would go a long way toward mitigating the...

"Argh!" the four nearest enemies screamed as they rushed him, raising short curved swords and what looked like a crescent wrench.

7 damage received.

6 damage received.

9 damage received.

14 damage received.

Max was knocked back by the flurry of blows pelting him from all sides. He tried to shield himself with his arms as he backed off into the smoke.

"You idiot!" Trina yelled. "You never used the salve!"

Max looked at her, struck dumb. She was right... he really should have.

Then the wrench appeared from the smoke and cracked right into the center of his skull.

22 damage received.

Max was knocked down, dazed. Why wasn't Trina using her ability? Couldn't she do anything?

"Trina..." he called. But the smoke in the ship was dissipating enough for Max to see that they all wore goggles over their eyes and scarves around their necks to block out the smoke. Max could see something else too: They all looked like pirates.

"Get him boys!" the female pirate called, raising the wrench high over her head. "It's just a skeleton and a necro."

"I am NOT a necromancer!" Trina called. The remaining three men were surrounding her.

I suppose I have to do something. But you're putting me right back after this.

Max tried to turn over but a boot came down on his back, pinning him to the deck.

“Now hold still while I smash that pretty skull a' yours,” Shaena said with a cackle.

There was a loud hiss and the ship was filled with something much darker than smoke. It was like ink from a well, but airborne and floating through the corridor at an incredible rate.

“Argh! I can't see!” One of the pirates yelled as he swung his sword at Trina, who ducked it easily. Then she ran over and put a shoulder into the woman with the wrench, knocking her back into the wall of corridor.

As the boot released Max was able to scramble backward, almost running into the snake who was silently sliding by to his left. It was incredible. It looked like someone had filled the entire ship with black paint... yet Max could somehow see through it perfectly. Each enemy was highlighted in white and each friend, including Trina and the snake, were gray.

Up front the battering ram finally smashed through the door to the bridge with a loud crash but that was followed by a lot of hissing.

Bite!

Bite!

Bite!

Bite!

The tiny crawlers went wild, flinging themselves from the ceiling of the bridge on to the pirates outside the door. As small as they still were, they might have been in trouble except that now none of the pirates could see.

“Everyone out!” their leader called. “Now!”

Amazingly, all the pirates turned as one and headed directly for the cargo bay door. Instead of attacking them, Max backed up against the wall, letting them pass.

The serpent and crawlers caught his intention to let them disengage right away, but not Trina, she was still fighting hand to hand with the woman with the wrench, trying to jam her knife into her enemy's thigh.

Max grabbed the back of her robe, pulling her away. “Let her go Trina,” he said. “I think they've had enough.”

“No I haven't!” the pirate sneered in Trina's face. “She has!” she yelled and raised her wrench high.

Max's Gloom Asp thumped the pirate on the head with his tail, stunning her.

“You are not to be underestimated in combat,” Max said to it.

Are we done?

“Yes, drag her out for me and I'll call you back.”

Thank you.

The snake grabbed the female pirate's shirt in its mouth and began dragging her out. It wasn't necessary to pick up the wrench because it was attached to her waist by a thick braided rope.

"Alright. So I guess it's time for parlay," Max said. "Oh and... I'll take that salve."

Trina's mask looked right at him. He could feel the heat of her glare, right through it.

Max was rubbing the last of the salve on his upper arm. Charred black flesh, remnants of his potion generated human body, was coming off on his fingers but not enough to make any difference. That actually made him wonder how he was supposed to wash this crap off his bones at all? Maybe dirty water would do it but he couldn't use soap could he? Definitely a question for the future. Maybe Khilen would know, he thought as he approached the tall man standing in the open area between the two landed airships.

Health restored.

The pirate leader was flanked by two others, each holding a short curved sword, like a pirate cutlass. The leader had a huge two handed curved sword hanging on his back. No wonder he hadn't taken part in the battle inside the Midnight.

Other pirates were dragging wounded comrades to their ship.

A human head popped out of the other ship. "Capn', I got the fire stopped, but there's a lot of stuff broke in here. I need Shaena."

The leader nodded, casting his dark blue eyes to where Max's Gloom asp had dropped the woman with the wrench.

Max held out a hand to where the snake was coiled and waiting. "Reggie, come back."

Thank you.

There was a poof of smoke and the cattan with the snake symbol reappeared in his hand. Max stored it.

Dark Summoner unlocked.

Whoa! What was this? He'd have to look into that one when he got a chance. It sounded cool!

"As a gesture of good will, we can help your wounded," Max said. "I'm gonna go out on a limb here and guess those guys are all poisoned and paralyzed."

The pirate leader frowned. "When Gent and the others told me they'd fought some kid in the market and he beat them up with a broomstick... I was surprised. Never crossed my mind that you'd be... whatever you are."

"Do you want us to help your people or not?" Max asked.

The man nodded. He was tall, with the chiseled features Max had come to expect from the higher level light people, but with an unkempt beard that ringed his strong chin. He wore solid looking reinforced black leather armor ringed with multiple belts and pouches, though all of it it had seen

seen better days. A tattered gray cape hung from his back though it too seemed to be made more of holes than of cloth.

"I'm Caerd Bannon, leader of The Black Skull Raiders," the man said.

"Ha!" Max said, pointing at his own skull. "That's funny... cuz they burned all my skin off so now I look like this. Do you think it means we're destined to be best friends?"

Caerd frowned. "No."

Max elbowed Trina. "Come on... don't you think it's funny?" he asked, looking over at her. She was just standing there, her mask quivering a bit, as if frozen. "Hey!" he said, knocking her with his elbow again. "You Ok?"

"Uh.. what?" she asked, looking over at him.

She completely missed the joke. "Can you heal the pirates of their conditions?"

Trina nodded. "Uh... yeah," she replied, her mask was back pointing at Caerd.

"Can you also call off whatever creature is destroying my ship?" Caerd asked, folding his arms. "It's the last one we have."

Max nodded. "Sure. I have a feeling I know who it is," he took a couple steps toward the other airship and cupped his skeletal hands to his mouth. "SCRUFF! Come out of there!"

There was a clang from inside the ship and someone screamed. A few seconds later Scruff squirmed out a porthole half way up the pirate airship. He then rolled down the side like one of those sticky octopus toys.

Break ship, Bite pirates.

Good job Scruff, Max thought. It appeared the creature had single-handedly delayed the pirates enough to prevent them from killing Mytten and stealing the ship, and he didn't even look any worse for wear. You're my hero Scruff, he added.

We win!

That's right buddy. We sure did.

When Max turned back, Trina was still standing there. Her hands were clasped together in front of her, like rubbing each other. What the hell was going on with her?

“Trina!” he yelled.

“Huh?” she said, startled. “What!?”

“Help. The. Pirates,” Max said, again.

Trina's mask pointed at him for a moment. “Oh... sure,” she said, finally moving to make it happen.

Max shrugged and looked back at Caerd. “She's a doctor... You know, they can be a little slow.”

Caerd frowned. “What are you?” he asked.

“I'm Max,” he said as Scruff finally finished clambering across the grass to Max's leg where he proceeded to climb up to his shoulder. "Technically my name is: Boneknight. But now that fate has declared us to be best friends forever, you might as well call me by my first name."

The pirate leader sighed. "I don't mean your name. I mean your class. You used a staff before but you also have all manner of creatures that follow your commands."

"When they want to, yeah," Max replied. He would have to have a chat with that snake, figure out his deal.

"Are you a Breeder or.. something else?" Caerd asked.

"Something else," Max said.

"Augh! Aaauuuugh!" cried a female voice.

Max looked over to see Shaena backing away as she pawed two fat leeches from her cheeks.

"You didn't have to put them on her face," Max said, crossing his arms.

"Yes I did," Trina replied sullenly.

What was up with Trina? "Just use the antidotes on the others. You were going to make more right?"

Trina nodded slowly, her bird-like mask bobbing up and down like she was listening to reggae.

"Shaena, Vicki's waiting for you inside. The ship's a mess," Caerd said.

"Of course it is!" Shaena snapped as she clambered to her feet. "It always is!" she pointed at Trina. "You just keep that creepy girl and her leeches away from me!"

"I haven't seen a dark being with power like yours in some time," Caerd said, ignoring Shaena and turning back to Max. "They'll be coming for you."

Max waved his hand. "They already are. Look, I don't want enemies among the dark. You guys tried to steal my ship but you're pirates. I get that. Nobody died, so as far as I'm concerned no harm no foul. We'll heal you up and you'll be on your way, right?"

Caerd looked at the Midnight before turning his eyes back to Max. "Where are you going in that stolen Kestrian Gyre falcon?"

"That's not something I'm willing to discuss with the guy who just tried to steal it," Max replied.

"A pity," Caerd said, running a gloved hand along his thin beard. "That's a good ship. Fast, well armed, with enough of a hold to make off with real wealth. The Kestrians are well trained and they protect their ships with their lives. I've wanted one for years but never had the chance. I'm impressed."

"And?" Max asked.

"And... I'd like to ask for your help," the pirate captain said.

There it was. "Doing what?" he asked.

"A job," Caerd replied.

"Air piracy?"

"Of course," Caerd said.

"As tempting as that is," Max said. "I have an important meeting I don't want to be late for. Also, I don't know if you've noticed, but there are only two of us."

"Two of you who overpowered my entire crew by yourselves."

"Most of that was the critters," Max said, patting Scruff on the head.

"Is that a dungeon crawler?" Caerd asked.

Max nodded.

"You know that's going to get enormous right?"

Max shrugged. "I hope so," he said. "I'm kind of a kaiju groupie."

"Is he always like this?" Caerd asked, turning toward Trina. "It's like he speaks in riddles."

Trina just stood there, like she was frozen.

Caerd frowned and turned back to Max. "Well?"

"I don't think so," Max said.

"With your abilities we'd have an easy time of it. The Reylosian regulars are weak. They'd be easy prey for us if our ship wasn't as old and beat up as she is. I love her, she's done a lot for me, for us... but I need something better and with your help we could do it. It wouldn't be as good as your falcon, but close."

"Yeah? I hear what you want from this arrangement, but what do we get out of it?" Max asked.

10

A MEAN GIRL AND A NICE ONE

"So... How about it?" he said, smiling as he leaned in closer to her. His teeth were perfect, just like everything else about him. Even his breath smelled good, like those round pink mints her grandmother always kept in a little glass jar on the shelf of her dining room hutch.

Brittney smiled back, finding it hard to contain her excitement. "I... think I could pencil you in," she replied.

"My airship is waiting," he said, "waiting for a girl like you, as am I."

It was corny, but made her melt just the same. There was something about a man lusting over her that made Brittney just want to squeal. It had always been that way.

"But what will your noble wife say?" she asked, prolonging the interaction, just so she could enjoy it for a little longer. She was going to go to the airship, there was no question, she just wanted to give the appearance of being hard to get, on principle. It was more fun that way.

His bright golden eyes never left hers. "She has no interest in my affairs, nor I hers. I like it that way and so does she."

"I see," Brittney replied, placing a hand on his thick chest. This man was the commander of the Hierarch's council guard, a Guardian with a great deal of vitality and strength, enough that she could feel it tingling on her fingers. Time with him would be very enjoyable.

He was leaning in even further, his cherry red lips coming closer to her as curled locks of thick brown hair rolled forward to frame their embrace.

Brittney's lips were trembling with anticipation.

"Here you are!" a high pitched voice crowed.

Brittney jolted upright, smacking her forehead into the Guardian's nose. There was a crunch.

"OW!" he cried, bounding back, slapping both hands over his face. Pinkish blood began gushing from between the fingers. "Wh... why did you do that?!"

Brittney glared at Vita who was currently flapping nearby by with her little paws clasped together angrily.

"I told you I was just going to give my report and then we were to meet in the portal room in the north tower," the tiny angel said. "This is NOT the north tower!"

"I KNOW it's not!" Brittney snapped.

"Who are you talking to?" the Guardian asked, then his eyes widened. "Y-you're a sikari!"

Brittney waved her hand. "It's fine."

He was already backing away. "I... I'm sorry. This was a mistake."

"No! Firian, wait!" she called but he was already gone.

Brittney's fingers clenched. She slammed a fist into the stone wall nearby, pulverizing a hole into the wall with a loud crack.

"Feel better?" Vita asked. "You're not supposed to be seducing the men here. You have a job to do."

"What if I don't care?" Brittney said.

Vita shook her tiny fluffy head. "Wrong answer. You know what he'll say."

Brittney scowled, turning away. "Yeah."

"Now put on your armor," Vita said. "I'll track the skeleton with my divining spell."

"Ugh!" Brittney said, switching her equipment. "I never get to enjoy myself anymore."

"You're not here to enjoy yourself. You're a sikari," Vita replied. "Here we go."

Brittney rolled her eyes. There was a flash of white smoke and suddenly they were at the edge of a town on the side of a mountain.

"Where the hell is this crap hole?" Brittney said with a snort.

“It's the town of Rose on the outskirts of the Reylosian kingdom,” Vita said.

“Are you sure he's here?” Brittney asked.

“I'm not a blood hound!” Vita replied, sounding annoyed. “I told you, I used divination. It gets us close, but it's rarely on the mark.”

Brittney grimaced. “Whatever. If you can't tell me if he's here, what can you tell me about this town?” she asked as she approached the gate. Black smoke was rising in the distance.

“There's not much to say,” Vita replied. “The town was constructed a long time ago, to mark the edge of the kingdom and for no other reason. It's otherwise useless and serves only to take resources from other parts of the kingdom,” said the voice. “At least that's what the Reylosian archives say about it.”

“Mmm Hmm,” Brittney said.

Two Reylosian guards stood in her way with a closed gate behind them. To either side of the gate were a series of poles with decapitated heads on them. The left side was a goblin head and a werewolf, and on the right were two orcs.

“State your business in Reylos!”

“I am Breylara, Sikari to the goddess,” she said. “Now make way before I cut off your heads and add them to your little display here.”

The guard on the left lowered his spear. "Sikari my ass," he said. "Those don't exist. That's just a superstition."

His friend stopped him, putting a hand on his chest as he eyed Brittney. "Think what happened today Bennar, best to be safe than sorry."

"Your buddy's right," Brittney said, raising an eyebrow. "I'm looking for an unholy abomination, a skeleton."

Both men's eyes widened with fear.

"T-t-talk to Nath," one said as he pulled open the gate. "He's been here... with a whole load a' his friends."

"I will," Brittney said, stepping past them.

"Sounds promising," said Vita.

"Yeah, it does, doesn't it?" Brittney replied, really wishing she was anyplace else, that gorgeous Guardian's airship for instance.

After asking around she found Nath with a group of ten others sifting through the rubble of a guardhouse on the south wall.

"Well?" she asked. "I was told you'd be able to tell me about a skeleton."

Nath eyed her. "Maybe, if you'll agree to dinner with me I'll consider it," he said, smiling and winking.

Brittney sneered. This guy wasn't rich or hot, he was a loser from a podunk town in the middle of nowhere. Her right hand shot out and grasped him by the throat. She lifted him from the ground and held him there, a foot up, for a count of thirty as his fingers fought to pry hers away from his flesh and his legs kicked and his eyes bulged. Then she dropped him.

"I won't ask again," she said.

Nath coughed, rubbing at his throat. "I'm... sorry..."

Her eyebrows raised slightly.

"Yes... Of course...the skeleton," he said. "He... entered the city this morning. He was pretending to be a human. He tried to steal from a shop but we caught him and burned him alive. I thought that was the end of it."

Brittney chuckled, casting her eyes around at the destroyed guardhouse and a massive chunk missing from one of the walls. "And then?"

"He returned... with an army! Legions of skeleton warriors marched on us. We fought bravely but they used magic to destroy our walls and force our surrender."

"Do you think he's a Dark summoner, a Necromancer?" Vita wondered.

"I doubt it," Brittney said, a dagger appearing in her hand. "Tell me the truth, or I'll flay the skin from your face, one strip at a time."

The man's eyes widened.

"The truth," Brittney said. "Or perhaps... I should start with what little you have between your legs."

"Ok!" the guard blurted. "It was just one skeleton... I think he's a Dark Mage. He was powerful. He had a girl with him too. Someone said she could heal the sick."

"You never cease to amaze me," Vita said with some admiration.

"Now we're making progress," Brittney said. "Next you're going to tell me where they came from and where they went."

~

"What do you need?"

"That's the thing," Max replied. "We got pretty much everything we needed from that town. We're self sufficient from here on out."

"I wish you'd tell me where you're going. Getting around in a stolen ship isn't easy. Every kingdom has their own rules about ship markings and flags. You're already breaking about six of them right now," he ran a hand through his hair, thinking. "That ship is new and you haven't repainted it, so you probably just stole it. You won't be going back to the east or anywhere near Kestria and I don't blame you. There's nothing south but mountains, trees, and ice so you're either going north, through Reylos and about ten other petty kingdoms, or west, through the mountains toward the ocean, probably the most dangerous choice of all. No matter which you choose there are problems. I can help you find the best route. I've been everywhere the skies have to offer and stolen from kingdoms on every continent."

"If I help you get a ship," Max said.

"Yes."

"We'll do it!" Trina blurted. She was now standing next to Max. When had that happened?

Max looked at her. "No, we won't."

"Yes! He's right," Trina said. "We don't know anything about long distance air travel. And if we want to get over the ocean we-"

"Oh ho! Crossing the Hylan Ocean is it? You're crazier than I thought!" Caerd said.

The pirate to Caerd's right, a short man with long hair and spectacles spoke up for the first time. "You know, you'll... you'll need every filgreth of that ship's cargo full of fuel right?"

"That's a good point Dag," Caerd said. "And where were you planning to get that, Mr. Boneknight?"

"I said you could call me Max," he said.

"Maybe Lord Boneknight?" said the other pirate to Caerd's left.

At this Caerd raised an eyebrow.

The man pointed. "He's wearin' a signet ring... ya see?"

Caerd frowned. "I say again sir, who exactly are you?"

Max stepped back. "No one of consequence. Just your average, everyday, run of the mill skeleton. Trina, tell them."

Trina said nothing. She just stood there, her mask pointed at Caerd.

Scruff hissed. The pirates to either side of Caerd took a half step back.

"You tell em' scruff," Max said, folding his arms.

"Will you help us?" Caerd asked.

"What level are you?" Max replied.

"Three," Caerd said, "Smuggler skill fifteen. Highest on the ship. It's why I'm the captain."

Max just stared for a second. "I'll think about it."

"Alright then," Caerd said. "We'll be moored at our base on half peak for the next day. It's straight west but only visible from the southern side. If you keep to the south of the ridge you can't miss it. Come find us if you decide it's worth it to you."

The pirates packed up and their ship took off, still smoking a little as it limped away. When it finally disappeared behind the mountain Max turned to Trina.

"What's up?"

"Huh?" she asked.

"Is there something wrong with you?" he asked.

"Do you think... he's dating that wrench girl?" Trina asked absently.

Max looked at Scruff who shrugged, then he rubbed a black charred hand against the front of his skull.

"I thought you hated relationships," he said.

"Huh?" she asked, her mask tilting in his direction. "Did you say something?"

"Nevermind," he said.

A group of trees cracked to Max's left as a huge reptilian head emerged from a stand of trees.

"Are they gone?" Rik asked.

"Oh! Rik!" Trina said. "I still have to make the powder for you." Then she ran back to the ship.

Max took the time while Trina was making the preparations for surgery to check on Mytten, who was a little shaken up but not hurt. Neither were the mini scruff's. Max was kind of annoyed with himself for forgetting to bring some offal home from that pit the townies threw him into. Now that he was a Breeder again they all sung to him of their endless hunger. They were dying from it, or that's what it sounded like.

Yeah, that would have to go on the list too. They'd earned it.

Trina appeared sometime later, her gloved hands steaming from hot water, with a tray covered in small sharp instruments.

"Yeah... I'm just gonna stay inside... you don't really need me for this do you?" he asked her. Just the thought of slashing through the dragon's wing skin, made his stomach churn... not that he actually had a stomach, but the feeling was there nonetheless.

"No, I don't," she said. "But when I'm done we're talking."

"Is this about the pirates?" he asked.

"Of course it is!" she said. "Caerd is right. We don't know a safe way over the water and we don't know if we'll have enough fuel to keep the ship aloft."

"OR," Max said. "He could be tricking us in order to get his hands on our ship."

"Nonsense," she said.

"Don't forget Trina, even though our levels are much higher than theirs, they almost took us down there. If it wasn't for Reggie's inky whatever it was... we could have lost."

"No!" Trina said, walking away. "That was your fault. If you hadn't stood there like an idiot trying to figure out what class to pick and used the last salve when I said to, it would have been fine."

Max grumbled, she had a point. "I don't trust them."

"We're not done talking about this!" she called as she walked down the ramp. "Ah! There you are... No don't worry it'll be over before you..."

And she was gone. Max was left feeling hollow. She was right about the salve and the class change. He'd been overconfident. That tended to happen after wrecking an entire town and all their guards on your own. He couldn't let it become a habit. Tesh was only one Sun Paladin from one Order. There would be more. The Kestrians were likely coming for him as well and there was no telling what horrors awaited them in Reylos or Gelra. He had to be careful. He had to think things through and be prepared.

Number one, that meant coming up with a class that could take hits and function on the front line. Though, honestly he'd already decided on that back at the shop.

He walked over into one of the three small side cabins in the ship. Trina was using this one for storing her vials, but there was only one small pack in there right now and pieces of what used to be a wooden chair. Max kicked the wood out of the way, making some space.

"Ok, first... I need to switch back to Dark Mage," he said. "Oh and Scruff, you should stay out in the hall."

Scruff dropped from his shoulder and backed off, heading out of the room.

Eat.

There was a sort of intensity to the word as it formed in Max's mind, giving him the distinct impression Scruff was sulking.

"I know! I promise, we'll find you something on the way. Believe me... if there's one thing that always seems to find me in this world, it's carnage," Max said as he brought up his equipment screen and unequipped the dark leather and the drain sword.

He turned toward the door just to make sure no one was there while he was just bones. He wasn't sure why, maybe it was that he caught some movement, but his eyes drifted up to the top of the doorway. There, hanging from the ceiling, was an enormous hairy spider.

"Augh!" Max said, tripping backward and landing on his pelvis in the center of the pile of broken chair bits.

Heya.

"Mytten!" Max yelled. "Don't do that!"

Do what? The ceiling in this ship has a metal plate with little circular holes in it. It's perfect for walking. My claws fit right in.

Max sighed, standing back up. "And dropping on unsuspecting skeletons?"

Only if they deserve it.

He looked up at her. "What's that supposed to mean?"

You're planning on leaving the pirates.

"Yes... well... maybe. They're a risky bet. Their captain just lied to me. He said he's a Smuggler but he's carrying a two handed sword. Only the ambition classes can use those, Smuggler is wanderlust."

Do you blame him? You're a powerful undead who bested his entire crew. To him you must be terrifying.

She had a point with that one. "Not only that, we'd be going out of our way to help them out, not knowing if we'll get anything in return."

You always do that. You helped the goblins, you helped the spider folk, and you helped the orcs.

"Yeah... and I always get into trouble because of it too. I'm running out of time Mytten. Who knows how hard it'll be to find her once we cross the ocean? I sure don't," he said. "Now let me be, I need to think about this Sleep rune."

I think you should reconsider. If only because it's funny watching Trina goggle at their captain.

"Hmmm?" Max replied. He wasn't really listening anymore, he was thinking about his last attempt to cast the Sleep spell as a rune.

11

A NIGHTMARE AND SOME BACON

Max brought up the class selection screen to chose Dark Mage. Dark Summoner was there, on the bottom next to Dusk Rider and Gladiator. He had to admit, that new one sounded awesome. There would be time to try that out later, hopefully. He was in the middle of something here.

Max chose Dark Mage. A wave of nausea followed but it passed in only a few seconds. He didn't bother equipping the hood and boots, they wouldn't help with the spell.

Good luck Max. Don't blow yourself up.

"Thanks Mytten," he said. "I think."

He might have to add the second set of words. He couldn't remember the level of Sleep, he thought it was in tier one but maybe not. The magic book had been clear about these things: Higher level spells required the second set of words and the highest spells, the third set. If you were casting Dark Magic, you said them in High demonic, if it was light magic: Angelic. Sleep was present in both schools according to the book, though the light called it 'Slumber'. Not that it mattered, he didn't know any Angelic anyway.

He squatted and pressed his palm to the floor in the center of the cabin. “Khüchiig en bairluul. minii khüsel zorigoor barig.”

He felt heat rush down the bones of his arm as the magic power pulled and a glowing circle was cast into the ground beneath him.

“Score!” he said, raising both skeletal arms. “The crowd goes wild! Haaaaaaa!”

Are you aware how silly you look doing that?

“Well aware. Actually, Mytten, I'm glad you're still here to see thi-”

Everything went dark.

The first sound Max heard was the clinking of chains. Looking around, he found that he was in a long hallway. It reminded him of a hospital and not a good one, the kind where they filled people with drugs and locked them up forever. There were doors all up and down the hall, each had viewing portals with bars and golden glowing magical wards etched into them. Thick locks ran up and down each one and they too were covered with hot glowing magic.

The sound was coming from from up ahead. Two men were standing in front of a doorway. They wore white robes with flat hats that covered their faces except for a single slit for their eyes like a demented mixture of hospital orderlies and torturers. The door was open and someone was coming out of it, someone in chains.

Everything looked dim here. It was like he was viewing an old dirty reel of film recorded decades before. Except it wasn't from the past, no, this was happening right now. He didn't know how he knew that but he did, he felt it. He could feel something else too, a swell in his heart.

Max stepped forward, trying to see who was coming out of the door but he knew who it was even before he saw her.

Arinna!

Her head hung low, her dark hair creating a stark contrast with the white robe they'd put her in. Her eyes remained down as her handlers took her by the arms and dragged her down the hall. He couldn't see her face, but he knew it was her, as sure anything in his entire life.

"ARINNA!" Max yelled. But they ignored him. Arinna's head did not turn, it did not raise. Nor did her handler's react. They continued to drag her forward and she hung there between them limply, letting them pull her along.

Why? Why wasn't she fighting?

"Arinna?" Max called again, running up behind them. "What's wrong? What's happened to you?"

He reached out to grab the shoulder of one of the men.

"NO! DON'T TOUCH THEM!" a commanding voice shouted from behind him.

Max spun around.

Floating in space were two figures. One was a huge eyeless beast-like creature with horns and a wide sharp toothed grin. Though covered in hair and with no discernible ears or eyes, the monster had spider-like appendages that stuck out of its back giving it a truly horrifying appearance. Max had never seen anything like it before but floating next it was someone far more familiar.

“Vish!” Max exclaimed. “Where the hell have you been?”

Vish tried to answer but when his mouth opened he reacted as if someone stabbed him.

“He cannot answer you,” the beast said, though its mouth was not moving. “I will provide you the necessary information. “I brought him... so you would know he sent me.”

Vish waved at Max halfheartedly, before fading into nothingness.

Max looked to the creature. “Ok... First, what do I call you?”

“I am Darsana Zuud, the dream killer, demon of nightmares and fevered dreams,” the creature replied. “Vishellus has asked me to connect you... with her.”

Right! Arinna! Max turned around.

The two handlers were half way down the hall with her now, about to turn a corner. Max jogged to keep up. When he looked back, the creature was still there, exactly as close as before.

"So I'm dreaming?" Max asked.

"Yes," Darsana replied.

"But she can't hear me," Max said.

"No," Darsana replied.

"Why?"

"She's not dreaming," the demon said. "Only you are."

"How is that possible?" Max asked.

"In order to create a nightmare, I can show anything to a dreamer, even the truth. Sometimes, that's the most terrible thing there is," it said.

Max kept up behind the two men, wishing he could kick them and help her escape. "Why can't I help her?"

"If you touch them, they'll become aware of your presence, but you're dreaming so there is little you can do," Darsana replied.

Max looked back at the creature. "How do you know Vish?"

"We used to date," it said.

"Wait... so you're female?"

"Such things have little meaning for demons like Vish and myself... but yes," she replied.

"Uh... I see," Max said. "So where is this place? Where are they taking her?"

"This is a complex under the Fortress of Gelra," Darsana said. "As for the other... who can say? I am seeing this for the first time as well."

"How can you see this but Vish couldn't?"

"This place is strongly warded against dark magic but dreams do not belong to the dark or light."

The handlers had dragged Arinna around the corner and down another hall, this one had fewer doors, but they were just as heavily locked and warded.

"What's wrong with Vish? What's happened to him?"

"He's been imprisoned by the demon lords of the underworld. They rule as a council in the king's absence. They have weakened him and I believe when he is weak enough, they plan to eat him," Darsana said with a somber tone.

"That does not sound good," Max said.

"It's not," she said. "I asked him what I could do and he told me to find you and help you find her. I've been trying, but you don't sleep very often."

"I'm undead," Max said. "Whether that's a bug or a feature, I don't know."

The handlers paused at another door. Two more of their white suited brethren were waiting. One used a thick sliver key to unlock the door and the other pulled it open. The handlers dragged Arinna inside to a long table in the center of the room. The table had restraints for the neck, wrists, and feet. Along the wall several robed people stood, also in white, but they had a different bearing to them, an air of determination. At their center was a fat man with short curly hair. He wore a self satisfied smirk as the handlers placed Arinna on the table and began to strap her down.

"What's happening here?" Max asked. "What is this place?"

"I don't know for certain... except that many of those who work here have nightmares that this will be done to them," Darsana replied. "It has something to do with weakening."

"They're weakening her?" Max asked.

"She's already weaker than I have ever seen her," Darsana replied. "I weep for her, for us all."

"No... No... I have to make them stop," Max said. "I have to-"

Max sat up. Mytten was right in front of his face.

Welcome back.

The spider slapped him across the face with one of her legs.

"Hey!" Max replied. "What was that for?"

You were dreaming and crying out in your sleep. Are you alright?

"No," Max said, thinking about Arinna, about what they were doing to her. "Not even a little."

A HUGE STEAMING plate was slid in front of Raeg, piled high with northern shellfish, all his favorite kinds. A cup of salted cream was put down beside it.

"Your salad is on its way. Just a few more minutes," the waiter, a semi-transparent creature with long tentacles for arms, said.

"Uh... thanks!" Raeg replied, picking up one of his favorite mollusks and snapping it open with the smooth practiced movement he'd learned many years ago when crewing a net hauler in the Finner Sea. He dipped the meat in the cream and sucked it in between his teeth, savoring the rich briny flavor. "Ah... I haven't tasted that in more than twenty years!" he said. "How is it you got Finner Sea Grips and Ringer Crabs in this place?"

Vigolos smiled, one of those empty smiles where the mouth formed the right position but the eyes remained dead. "In this place food is a manifestation of spiritual power. What you're eating is whatever you want it to be, whatever you're the most hungry for. The more power available, the better the food."

Raeg sucked the meat from a cracked crab leg. "Sure tastes like real food."

"It is... to you," the dark elf replied. "What else matters?"

Raeg dipped a second lump of crab into the liquid cream before sucking it into his mouth. "I couldn't tell ya."

"Exactly. Feasts like this are the reward for a job well done. This one is free. I give it to help you recover after the strain of your transition, but from here on, you'll have to earn your keep," Vigolos said, leaning back in his booth.

Raeg sucked three more of the Sea Grip mollusks, reveling in the sweetness of the meat. The waiter had returned. He brought a re-fill for Raeg's Willern White ale and a gloriously large salad. He leaned over.

"So this is a Cobb salad? Which is the bacon?" he asked the waiter.

A tentacle reached out pointing to little reddish chunks of crispy meat.

"Oh... it does look like a cured meat," Raeg said.

"I told you," Vigolos said. "The eating establishments here can fabricate anything you can dream of, even things you've never had. Some are better than others, of course. Ted is one of the better cooks on this side of town."

The waiter bowed and left the table.

Raeg wiped his hands on a napkin and dug into the salad. The thing was so loaded with toppings you could barely even seen the green leaves beneath, but that was just fine. Flavors he'd never experienced exploded on his tongue. The rotten looking cheese was creamy and sour with a little bitterness but everything was bathed in a salty meaty sumptuousness coming from the chopped eggs, the bacon, and some kind of pungent sour sweet sauce.

"I... love... this," Raeg mumbled through a mouthful.

"Good," Vigolos replied. "Then you'll be happy to get to work so you can have more."

"Uh... yeah!" Raeg replied. "Who do I have to kill?"

Vigolos smiled again, but this time it was a real one. "I appreciate enthusiasm, I do. Your job is to find and eliminate problem souls. The official title is sanitation associate but the common name for your profession is: Char, because of what you do.

"And what's that?" Raeg asked through a mouthful of crab meat.

"Once a soul is apprehended and neutralized, they go into the animus furnace where they're burned."

"We burn em?" Raeg asked. "Why?"

"It's the proper way to dispose of trash," Vigolos replied with a sneer. "The burning collects spiritual power and you get a percentage of the power harvested." He spread his arms. "Making something like this possible."

Raeg nodded. "And they're bad souls?"

"The worst," Vigolos said. "You're a stronger candidate than I've had for a while. I'm not going to lie to you... I'm going to need you in the field right away. Training will be quick and dirty."

"I'm a hands on kind of guy," Raeg said as he ripped a leg from a crab and crushed the steaming shell between his fingers.

"I like to hear that. We have only two rules in this profession: Do what you're told and don't screw it up."

Raeg nodded. "I like it. It's simple," he said. "If what you're telling me about how strong I am is true, I should have no trouble makin' good on this arrangement," he frowned, thinking. "But... why am I so strong?" he asked as he cracked another crab shell.

"Why are you asking me?" the dark elf replied. "It's a result of your time when you were alive. You must have killed many enemies, probably strong ones. That is rare for those of dark these days."

"Hmmm..." Raeg replied. He had been doing a lot of fighting. But who and why? It was all foggy. "I'm having a hard time remembering it."

Vigolos waved his hand, smiling. "Consider yourself lucky," he said. "Many souls arrive here traumatized by their life or death, sometimes both. It's far better to let it go. It doesn't matter anyway, you're here now and you have a job to do."

"That weird spider thing with the mask told me I was in the line for souls with regret," Raeg said.

"Who doesn't have regrets from their life? I sure do, but there's no point whining about it. We're dead. We've got nothing to worry about anymore. Especially you, you've been chosen. This is an opportunity to grow in power and prestige here. Why, in time you could even become a lesser demon yourself. You wouldn't give that up would you?"

Raeg shook his head. "Hell no!" Actually, there was something else he wanted to know. "Oh... that demon who asked me questions. He wanted to know what I thought about the king and the scragger."

Vigolos raised a single black eyebrow. "And?"

"Why?"

Vigolos sighed, looking to the left and right before leaning in. "Alright... I'll explain a little. Basically, they're no longer welcome here, either of them. The king abandoned the dark and the glorified lesser demon you know as the scragger is, if anything, even worse. He's been smuggling resources out our lands for centuries, weakening us for no reason. Both of them have been declared enemies of the dark. The king has been gone for centuries but the other...well... he won't be a problem for much longer."

"Oh," Raeg said. "That's good."

"It's great! We're finally able to begin changing this place for the better. It really is a new day for the dark. However, that's where you come in, Raeg. We still have too many of the old guard around, slowing the pace of change, making everything harder. That's what Helran was talking about. We don't want any more Gazric lovers here."

Raeg nodded. "Me either."

"Excellent, now finish that up and I'll get you to work."

12

YO HO AND A BOTTLE OF GLUM

The Black Skull Pirates were waiting right where they said they'd be: moored on the southern side of a mountain peak. There was a little cave there. It was decided unanimously that one of them should stay and guard the ship, but Trina wanted to go.

"I'm the planner here," she'd argued but as soon as Max mentioned Caerd Trina had turned red and suddenly decided to put her mask on again. That was why Max was now climbing down the rope ladder that hung from the bottom of the ship alone, with out even Scruff hanging from his shoulder.

Shaena the wrench carrying pirate grabbed his ladder, steadying it as he put a boot to the ground. He'd switched back to Breeder for the meeting. Trina had agreed it was best the pirates didn't know about his other abilities. Even if he could trust them, the less others new about his powers or their destination, the better.

"Not showing up in your Dark Mage robe?" Shaena asked, a grin pulling at one corner of her mouth.

Max stared at her. Rats. "I don't know what you're talking about," he said as he dropped from the ladder to the stone.

"Don't bother denying it. Several of our guys saw you rampage through that place. We picked them up in town on the way back," she said. "Unless there's another black charred skeleton around."

Caerd was walking up behind her. "I told you I wanted to wait!"

"I couldn't stop myself!" she whined. "Who cares? It's not like you can read his expression!"

If he told them the other dark skeleton was his twin brother... would they buy it? Probably not. "I'm not really a Dark Mage. I just dabble in magic in my spare time. It's more of a hobby really," Max said. "Though, in the interest of trust, why don't you tell me why you lied to me about your class?"

Caerd paused, looking surprised. "I..."

"Smugglers can't use two-handed weapons," Max said. "Tell me another one."

The pirate leader shook his head. "Just come inside," he said and turned on his heel.

Max followed. Inside the cave were several empty circular containers of fuel, a bunch of hanging meat and some tables with equipment laid out on them. It was all very haphazard. It was a good thing Trina hadn't come, the disorganized nature of the place would have given her a second thing to be bothered about.

"The plan is pretty straight forward," Caerd said, leading Max over to a table in the corner. It had an oil fed lamp that cast light on a map. He took out a small knife and pointed to a line of mountains near the bottom of the map. "This is us. That's the city you exploded earlier today."

Max looked up. "I didn't explode it... I made a few minor renovations. It was stuffy in there, it needed air."

Shaena chuckled and Caerd stared at her, his blue eyes like shards of ice.

"Sorry," she said.

"I'm actually not very happy about that," Caerd said. "You made a huge mess for me. One that's far bigger than just a few downed guards and a destroyed tower. The Reylosians will assume the Dark Mage to be working with pirates-"

"Which I am, because you asked me to," Max interjected.

"-and that means we can't use this as a base anymore." he continued. "However, if you do your part, we can move on to greener pastures with a faster, stronger ship."

"Why should I?" Max asked. "You lied to me about your class. For all I know this could be some elaborate trick to set me up and take my ship."

"I'm a Tactician," the pirate said.

"Yeah?" Max asked. "I've read about that one. The brains of the battlefield, all about maneuvers and trickery. Doesn't exactly fill me with confidence."

Shaena slammed her wrench down on the table, leaving a huge dent in the wood. "You don't know anything, skeleton!" she snapped. "The captain has saved us countless times! Most of us wouldn't even be alive without him."

Caerd held up a hand. "Shaena, stop. He'll make up his own mind."

Max stood there for a moment, surveying the pirates. Most were working diligently, but their situation was obviously desperate. Everything in the lair was in disrepair, even worse than their dilapidated ship and most of the pirates looked tired and hungry. Despite that, they were still here, still following Caerd. Either he was a tyrant they feared, which didn't seem to be the case given the ease with which they addressed him and each other, or they were loyal because he treated them well.

"I need a guide to get me across the ocean and enough fuel to get across, quickly," Max said. "That's the price."

"Done," the pirate leader said. "If that's all you want, I'll make sure you get it. Fuel is part of the plan. Look here." He pointed his knife to a city on the coast. "This is the coastal city of Rey. They don't have a lot going on there. It's basically just a fuel depot for transport ships heading over the ocean to trade."

"Probably the most boring, insufferable place to ever be," Shaena said.

"True, but it's been the center of all our operations for years," Dag, the pirate with the spectacles said. "Our ship is so slow that we've had no choice but to return there over and over to steal fuel."

"So what, they got wise to your little racket?" Max asked.

"Yes," Caerd said. "The Reylosians recently stationed a heavy cutter... here," he pointed to the map north a bit. "It almost took us down two months ago,"

"The captain pulled an incredible maneuver," Shaena said.

"I was lucky," Caerd replied. "Lucky there was fog enough in the valley to hide us while we doubled back on them. Otherwise we'd all be dead."

"What do I need to do?" Max asked.

"We'll attack the depot, making sure to give the locals time to notify their reinforcements in the north." He pointed at Max. "Your ship will be above, hidden in the clouds. Then, when the cutter shows up you drop in on it. Like most ships they have a hatch on top. Kill everyone aboard, and land it at the depot. We'll then steal fuel and everything else that isn't nailed down."

"Or even things that are," Shaena said with a smile, hefting her wrench over her shoulder.

"What if there's no cloud cover?" Max asked.

"There is, there always is," Dag said. "It's a quirk of Rey, something about the climate there, it's always cloudy."

"Ah," Max said. "And I'm supposed to take out all the soldiers on that ship myself?"

"Do you want me to put ten armed pirates on your ship to help take it?" the pirate leader asked.

Max shook his head. "No... you have a point. What level are the Reylosians?"

"They are usually three, maybe four, but I've heard stories about this crew, there may be someone level five," Caerd said. "Can you handle that?"

"I suppose I have no choice," Max said. This was sounding like it might actually be easy. That alone was making him nervous. He should be extra careful going forward.

"Oh, actually," Max said, thinking. "Before I go... I have a couple things."

Caerd looked up from the map. "What?"

MAX CRAWLED BACK UP into the cabin and started pulling up the ladder behind him. Trina and Mytten were waiting for him. Trina was standing in the corridor tapping her foot with her arms crossed while Mytten was hanging from the ceiling, looking down from above placidly.

"Well?" Trina asked. "What are we doing?"

Scruff had appeared from a nearby cabin, his tentacles twitching. Behind him were the other smaller versions of him. They too were twitching with anticipation. How did they already know? Could they smell it?

Max yanked one last time, hauling up a big carcass the pirates had been hanging in the cool dry air of the mountain. It almost didn't make it through the hatch. He didn't even have time to move it before Scruff and his comrades launched themselves at it.

"You're welcome," Max said with a chuckle as he pulled the hatch closed and stood up. "We have to be at the city of Rey by tomorrow evening."

"Never heard of it," Trina said. "Is that even a real place?"

Max walked past her, heading down the corridor and past the final bulkhead to the mostly destroyed door to the bridge. "Hey Tela," he said.

"Hi Max!" Tela chirped. "How was your meeting?"

"It was great," Max said.

"That's wonderful!" Tela replied. "I'm so happy to hear that!"

Trina had followed Max into the bridge. "Was it really great?"

Max shook his head slowly. "Actually they want me to kill everyone on an airship for them so they can take it."

"They're Reylosians right?" Trina said. "If they're soldiers for the kingdom they'll be revived."

"I know," Max said. "That's not why it's a problem, as sad as that might be. It's a problem because it'll be close quarters fighting and my best class for that is brawler at skill level twenty-three. That's good, but not enough to take on a whole ship. If I use Breeder I have to put Mytten and the Scruffs at risk, not something I'm willing to do."

I wish to go. We'll fight them together!

Max turned to Mytten who was on the ceiling outside of the bridge. "No Mytten, I'm serious. You're not fully healed. If I let you die Cheren would come back from the dead and throttle me."

"What are you going to do then?" Trina asked. "Didn't you say you have something else?"

"I do. I could go with Gladiator, but I'm still not a fan. No... I bought some armor for Mercenary and we're going to give that a try."

Trina frowned. "But you'll be level one won't you?"

Max held up a single boney finger. "Ah... perhaps not. Tela, can you fly two mountains to the west and then fly down the southern mountain side. We're looking for a rocky grotto."

"Sure!" Tela said. The airship started moving immediately.

"Great, let me know when we're there," Max said and paused, looking at Trina. "You might want to turn around."

"Oh! Yes!" Trina said and ran right out of the bridge.

Max unequipped his leather armor and changed to the selection screen. He pressed: Mercenary.

His vision swam and he fell to his knees.

"Are you alright?" Trina asked, peeking back in.

"Yeah," Max squeaked. This wasn't the worst class change sickness he'd felt... but it was close. His stomach was churning and there was a throbbing inside his skull that made it feel like something in there was trying to get out with a big hammer. Maybe changing so many times in a day hadn't been such a great idea. He wavered, almost falling to all fours, but then he used the door to pull himself up. "I just need... to get... to the sleep sign."

"No you don't," Trina said as she smacked him with a little bag of white powder.

Everything went dark.

Max was in the Gelra complex again. He could tell immediately from the sterile lighting and the smooth walls. But where was Arinna? He looked around, turning a circle. She wasn't there. He was alone in the hall, surrounded by dozens of locked, warded doors. She was probably in one of them, but which? Did he had time to check them? Probably not.

"I SEE YOU!"

Max jumped, backing up against a the wall between two of the doors.

"YOU DON'T BELONG HERE!" a voice said. No, it wasn't not a voice, it was more like a feeling. A screaming pain inside his skull, full of condemnation.

"Uh... sorry?" Max said. Immediately he wished he could take it back. Never had saying something felt so wrong. Whatever he was talking to hated him. It hated everything he stood for. He could feel it, like the heat of that damned flash oven back at the coffee shop. He hadn't thought of that place in weeks, why was he thinking about it now?

"THIS IS FORBIDDEN!"

Max sat up.

Trina and Mytten were hanging over him. "Oh... Thank you for waking me up... I-"

You wouldn't wake. I hit you a lot.

"You've been out for two hours," Trina said. "We tried everything. Mytten hit you a lot."

"It felt like it was only a few seconds... I was..." He didn't know how to describe it. Maybe... hunted? Yes! It felt exactly like he was being hunted, by something terrifying.

"You dreamed?" Trina asked.

Max nodded. "It's the second time. Before, while you were sewing up that dragon, I met someone, they showed me Arinna. She's not well. That's why I decided to meet with the pirates. We need to get across the ocean as fast as possible. They're doing things to her, terrible things."

Trina scowled at him. "That's why you changed your mind. You should have told me!"

"I know... This time though, it was different. It was the same place but Arinna wasn't there and someone was yelling at me, someone who hated me."

Trina put a finger to he chin. "The old stories say that the land of dreams is a middle ground, a place where light and dark both go. For a long time it meant the conflict went there too, but it caused untold chaos as the war spread into the dreams of sleepers so Cerathia and Gazric signed an agreement inked in their own blood. Only two were allowed to go there, a demon to create nightmares and an angel to create visions of triumph."

"Dasana," Max said.

"Yes... She's the demon of nightmares," Trina said. "People don't understand how important those are. We need to feel afraid sometimes. It keeps us safe, on our toes."

"So the one who hated me was..."

"Sapana," Trina said. "The angel of dreams."

"I didn't see her, but she sounded... scary," Max said.

"I don't know much about her," Trina said with a shrug. "But a good rule of thumb is that if you aren't a god or a demon, you don't want to tangle with an angel."

"I get that," Max said. "I really do." He looked around. "Are we there yet?" he asked.

For about an hour.

"Yes," Trina said. "Now put on your equipment!"

Max looked down to where a blanket had been thrown over his naked bones. "Right," he said and brought up the inventory screen and equipped all the pieces of his new Mercenary armor. It was time to get some levels.

13

SHELL SHOCKED AND HORRIFIED

Max was taking a break, sitting on a rock, just taking in the idyllic scenery stretching out before him. The spray from the waterfall to his rear was causing a half-rainbow to arc out into the rocky ravine that ran down the side of the mountain. Trees grew out of the sides of the ravine, clinging to the boulders like green leaved barnacles. They, like the rocks they were attached to, were constantly bathed in spray from the waterfall, causing them to glitter in the golden afternoon light of the distant setting sun, just visible over a peak to his west.

There was no real reason for him to take a break. He didn't get tired really. He was still an undead skeleton after all and impervious to hunger or fatigue. It felt good though, it soothed him. He'd been beating on that tortoise all day long with Trina intermittently harassing him for it and now it just felt like it was time for a rest.

"Hisssss," the tortoise said, snapping in his general direction for the thousandth time.

"I'll get back to you in a minute," Max said. "I'm trying to have a moment."

"Hisssssssss," the tortoise replied, narrowing its tiny eyes angrily.

The pirates had told him the creatures were here, giant tortoises, light aligned, with delicious flesh, or so they said. Their skin was too tough and their damage resistance far too high to actually hurt them with weapons. This is why the pirates resorted to trickery, digging large pits to push the creatures into, then filling the pits with water. It was sneaky and underhanded, but effective and honestly it reminded Max a little of his first victory against Tesh in the river. Sometimes you gotta do whatever it takes to survive.

Max had done something similar except his hole was only big enough to keep the tortoise's legs hanging, making it immobile.

1 damage received.

"Ow," Max said. The Sun steel scale armor had pretty good coverage but every once in a while the pure spray from the waterfall would build up enough on his exposed face bones, to do a point of damage. It turned out wearing light aligned armor had its uses. If he closed the visor, he took no damage at all, but that made it a little harder to see. Not that he didn't like it, the helmet reminded him a little of a football helmet, and the visor opening was well designed to give good visibility in a wide area. Nobody was attacking him now though, so there was no point.

"Hissssss," the tortoise said.

"Yeah I know you wish you could bite me up good," he replied to the captured creature.

"Are you just going to chat with it now?" Trina called down from above.

Max looked up to where the rope ladder hung. At its top was the open hatch and Trina's face, with a wry expression.

"Maybe I will," Max said. "He's very refined, for a tortoise."

"Hissssssssssss," the tortoise replied. Max couldn't help but take it as an insult.

"I was being nice!" Max said to it.

"When will you be done? We should leave soon!" Trina yelled down.

"Did you get any skill levels making the rest of our potions?"

"Seven!" she replied. "And..."

"Nice!" Max said. " And what?"

Trina shook her head. "Nothing, never mind. How many did you get?"

Max shrugged. "I have no idea. Maybe zero."

"That would make your whole day a huge waste of time," Trina said.

Max looked back at the sunset through the mist. “Not a complete waste.” As beautiful as it was, he kept thinking of Arinna. That's what had kept him hacking at the tortoise with Raeg's black iron axe all day long. He didn't want to break his drain sword and Raeg's hand made axe had sentimental value, so black iron it was. The thing handled pretty well too.

Max sighed, leaning forward to get up. “Alright... I'll just whack old lumpy a couple more times and be on my way.”

Unfortunately, his boot slipped on the wet surface of the rock and he landed on his back, his helmet clanging against the big rock beneath him before he slid all the way down to the ground.

From above he heard Trina laughing.

Max shook his head. At least he hadn't taken any damage.

“Mmmmmm whoooooo... gooooes therrrrre?” a deep voice said. It sounded like it was coming from everywhere at once. Then the ground started to move and lift and Max was tossed ten feet back ward. He landed right next to Lumpy the Tortoise who promptly bit him on the arm.

3 damage received.

“Ow!” Max said, pulling himself free of the creature's vise-like beak. “Though I admit... I had that coming.”

A giant head rose out of the dirt. What Max had taken to be a rock was in fact the shell of a much larger tortoise. The great head looked from Max to the smaller immobilized tortoise and back again.

"He'ssss doinnggg Whaaat?" the tortoise asked.

The two could talk? This was bad.

"Trina!" Max said, but before he'd even finished the word the tortoise raised his shell and head even more, slamming the top of its car-sized skull into the bottom of the airship with a loud clang. This knocked the whole ship off line. Max watched the ladder, which had before terminated just above the rock that turned out to be a shell, as it floated away out of reach

"Torrmentorrr! Vile Creature! I shall slayyyy theee!" the monster tortoise said as it slowly raised a stumpy front foot the size of an obese elephant and tried to bring it down on Max's head.

Max tried to scramble away but wearing armor and having mercenary skill level one didn't exactly make it easy. However, he did manage to roll into a crevice between two boulders. When the great front foot hit the ground above him like a two ton pile driver, the crevice helped him avoid any damage.

When the creature lifted its foot to inspect it, Max actually used the other tortoise's head to drag himself out of the rocks.

"Heyyyy! Commmme Baaack!" the giant called.

"Max! Here!" Trina said.

The ship was to his left now, re-positioned over a two hundred foot drop into the lower parts of the canyon. Trina was pointing to the ladder.

"Jump!"

Max ran up as close as he could. "No chance!" He yelled. "The armor is too heavy and I'm too slow."

"Haaaaa! Haaaaaaaaaa!" the giant tortoise crowed with satisfaction. "Yoooouuuu Caaaan't escaaaape... yourrrrrr doooooommm. Dieee!"

Max turned around to see a gigantic open maw coming right at him. Then something hit his back, making the scales of his Sun steel mail clink and he was jerked up and away.

"Aaaaaauuuuuuuggggghhh!" Max yelled as he dangled over the crevices and crags below.

"I'lllll Gettttt Youuuuuuu!" the tortoise hollered up at him.

When he looked up, Max saw Mytten. She'd shot a web at him and was now hauling him up with her back legs.

"Thank you!" he yelled up at her.

Anytime.

"Spiders," Max said, "are awesome."

~

MAX STOOD over the glowing symbol on the floor, hesitating hard. Twice now he'd used it and twice he'd been shown things that made him angry and terrified. Not just for himself, but for her. What was she going through now? What were they doing to her and more importantly: Why? What could they do now that they haven't done a thousand times before during her captivity? What was the point of further torture unless they were just sadists.

Tesh had been like that: addicted to causing pain to others. He'd reveled in his control over Max, and how easy it was to make him suffer. He'd built his equipment around causing pain and suffering, drawing out death until the last possible moment, it was his thing. Max had even met his wife and didn't get the feeling that she'd care that he was gone. She'd probably already found someone better, someone who might actually treat her like a human being.

Just go.

Max looked up and behind. Mytten was hanging from the ceiling there. "Easy for you to say," he replied. "You didn't see what they're doing to her."

Sometimes we have to do things we don't like.

"Are you my mom now?" Max asked the big hairy spider hanging behind him.

No.

He sighed. She was right.

"Trina... how long until we get to the city?" he called back through the doorway.

"For the last time, it'll be another thirty minutes. Now use the sleep sign to level up or switch back to Breeder or Dark Mage. I don't care!" Trina yelled back.

Max balled his fists. Fine. It'll be fine.

He stepped into the circle.

Maybe this time he wouldn't even see anyth-

Everything went blank.

Max woke up staring down. He couldn't move at all. It was like he'd been glued to the ceiling. There were many people below him, gathered into a large group. They wore long white robes and hats, they looked like mages, Light Mages. They were chanting something and holding their hands like they were praying.

No... that wasn't prayer, it was a focusing gesture used to control the release of only the most powerful spells. At the center of the crowd was a table draped with a white sheet that was covered with scores of written symbols in angelic writing. The sheet was draped over a shape that could only be one thing: a body.

"What's going on?" Max yelled at them. He struggled against whatever force was holding him. Fear seized him as he realized that it was probably her under that sheet, that it was Arinna!

Was she dead? Was that even possible?

"What have you done to her you bastards!" Max said, gritting his teeth. "I'll kill you!"

At that... there was a twitch on the table.

"She's moving! Stop her!" barked a voice from the corner. "Laras, re-cast the torpor! We just need her there for a few more seconds."

Max looked over.

A huge man with short curly hair wearing what looked like a glorified potato sack was standing in the corner. He was the one barking orders and gesturing with some kind of thin pipe.

Another mage was moving. "As you command," he replied, bringing up his hands.

"No! No!" Max shouted. "Stop it!"

There was something else in the room too, something malevolent. Two men with masks were standing next to glass tube with a golden cap. Inside a form was swimming, something like a fish, with long fins and golden glowing eyes.

The mage was chanting the spell.

"I said STOP!" Max screamed.

There was another jerk under the sheet, fingertips appeared at the top and slowly, as if in a daze, Arinna pulled the covering from her face. She was staring at him but not seeing him. Her eyes were empty, drugged.

"ARINNA!" he yelled, as hard as he could. "LOOK AT ME! SEE ME!"

Her eyes widened. Had she?

"I'M COMING! HOLD ON!"

Were her lips moving? Was he seeing things or was she trying to speak to him?

There was a flash as the White Mage's spell finished and washed over Arinna like a wave. Her eyes rolled back in her head and her fingers went limp.

"NOOO!" Max shouted as the mage came closer, entering the circle and pulling the sheet back over her.

The mage then moved the sheet, centering a slit in the middle. Two flaps that opened like... like those things they draped over patients during an operation!

"What are you doing to her! GET AWAY!" he said.

"It's time," the mage said, a thin knife appearing in his hand.

The two robed men brought the tank forward. The creature inside was wriggling to get out.

"No!" Max cried as he looked at it, as he realized what they were doing. "You can't..."

"You must go, now." It was the voice of Darsana, the nightmare demon and it had an urgency Max hadn't heard before. "She knows about you. She's coming."

"Go!" Darsana said as she appeared before him, this time not as a hairy beast-like creature but as a woman with thick dark hair and pure blue-green eyes tinged with a ring of red.

"I can't leave her here," Max said. "I can't."

"You must," Darsana replied and her palm touched his forehead.

Max awoke, gasping for breath, even though he had no lungs. Where was he? What was going on?

"Well?" Trina asked, standing in the door to the cabin.

"Huh?" Max replied.

Then a furry pedipalp slapped him in the face.

"I'm awake Mytten! Stop!" he said.

Sorry.

Max turned around to find the giant spider looming behind him, taking up most of the rest of the cabin. "No you aren't," he said.

Mytten bounced a little on her legs but did not reply.

"I thought so," he said.

"Wellllll?" Trina said again. "Did you get skill levels or not? We're here and pirates have already landed.

Max sat up, "They have?" he brought up his status display.

Status	Boneknight	Betrothed	
Level	20	Mercenary Skill	44
Health	495/495		
Magic	1/1	Affinity	Dark
Skills		Magic	
Rekindle, Vengeance		Dead Weight, Teeth of Fate, Void Crush, Flame, Chill...	
Strength	34	Attacks x 2	36
		Accuracy	85%
Agility	15	Defense	74
Vitality	33	Evasion	8%
		Magic Defense	12
Mind	20	Magic Evasion	9%

Skill level forty four?! His strength stat had definitely improved, by a lot, and that was with the minus ten! It felt good to have actual stats. His mind stat would be pretty ugly if it weren't for the rings, though, but that was to be expected for a front-line combat class. Brawler had been similar.

Ooh, and he'd gotten another ability. Hmm. Actually he hadn't. There wasn't a third ability there, the one from from before had changed. Blitz had been replaced by Vengeance. From what Max remembered, the earlier ability had to do with cutting your defense to raise your offense. He hadn't bothered with it when fighting the turtles because he hadn't actually wanted to do much damage. Power-leveling combat classes was all about hitting enemies as many times as possible, killing your target only slowed the process down.

This ability was similar, but better. It was an activated ability that did the same thing, but with a bonus based on the number of times he'd taken damage in a single combat. Huh, that could be useful against someone like that spear guy he'd met before. That guy could hit him three or four times in a row.

"Level forty-four, with a new ability," he said. "We're in business."

Trina sighed. "Good," she said. "I was getting worried..." her eyes unfocused as she stared off into the distance.

"What?" Max asked.

"Huh? Oh... I was just wondering if we'll see Captain Caerd,"

Mytten suddenly decided to exit the room, pushing past Trina in a way that nearly knocked her down.

"Hey!" Trina snapped, "Watch it you eight-legged... thing!"

Max stood up. "I'd refrain from calling Mytten names if I were you," he said. "She has really big fangs."

Trina frowned.

A slight pitching of the deck toward the front of the ship let them know it was slowing.

"You should come up front!" Tela said cheerily. "We're in position!"

14

RIPPED OFF AND DRIVEN INTO THE GROUND

Raeg ran through the street, water splashing under his boots as he rounded a corner and launched himself into the alley he found there. It was dark inside and the footsteps he'd been following had stopped, meaning that somewhere ahead his quarry was lying in wait.

Good.

He barreled head anyway and when the shine of reflected pink from the sign across the street outlined the edge of a long scythe, he ducked and rolled beneath it. Coming up just in time to smash his right fist into the gut of the creature swinging it.

"Ough," his enemy called out as his two long arms wrapped around his center. The scythe dropped to the ground with a clang.

Raeg seized the opportunity to slam his left fist into the creature's head, rocking it back on its heels before it fell on its backside, splashing in a puddle of the gray rain that almost always fell in the darker parts of the city. It was weird that things in the world of the dead were eerily similar to the land of the living but Raeg tried not to think about that. Every time he tried to think about the time before, his head started hurting.

"Please... No!" the creature said, backing up on all fours. A shaft of light from the street behind caught his face.

Human... or he looked human anyway.

"Sorry," Raeg said as he stepped forward and gripped the man by the throat, dragging him back to his feet, "but you're my meal ticket."

The man tried to fight but he was too weak. His left hand was scarred by some horrible burn that had left him with only two fingers which he used to grab at Raeg's arm while his other hand covered the chain about his neck and the prize that hung here. It was trivial to swat the fool's hand away and snatch the black tag that hung around his neck. Raeg yanked, snapping the chain.

"No!" the man pleaded. This time, as he spoke, the man's face partially disappeared revealing a skull, the face of a reaper. "You don't know what you're doing."

"I do," Raeg replied, "killing you." Then he touched the black tag to his own causing a flash of light that filled the entire alley.

The reaper dropped to the ground, stunned. Raeg put the black tag in the pouch he'd been given and then grabbed his target, throwing him over his shoulder.

It was funny, every time he saw one of those reaper skulls, there was a feeling of familiarity, but then it passed. Had he been a reaper once? Had he known one?

Better to put such things out of the mind. He was gonna eat tonight. That was what mattered.

"I'll take that," Yem said, holding out his clawed fingers.

Raeg turned around, "Sure." He didn't know his coworker had been so close or he wouldn't have put the tag in his pouch. It was always twice as hard to fish them out.

"Come on," Yem snapped with a sneer. "I don't have all night, scum."

"Here," Raeg said, placing it in the werewolf's hand. Yem might be the ugliest werewolf Raeg had ever seen. He was fat and shaggy, with matted fur everywhere. He didn't seem to care how he looked though and it didn't matter to Raeg.

What did annoy him, though, were the insults. He wasn't sure why Yem kept calling him names but he was getting pretty sick of it. He didn't know what the penalty was in the underworld for killing your coworker, but soon he might find out.

"Come on baldy, bring that bone bag. We gotta get back so I can eat. Plus... I worked hard today and I need a rest," Yem said.

"You didn't do shit," Raeg said, annoyed. "I did it all."

Yem pointed a clawed finger at him. "Shut up or I'll rip your arms off and eat your ugly human face!"

Raeg sneered. “Just try it, dog,” he replied.

Yem's eyes widened with what Raeg was sure had to be fear, but the werewolf smoothed it over quickly. “I was just kiddin' baldy.” he said as he turned and stalked along the wet street. “Let's go burn that bone bag. What's that make it today... ten?”

“Eleven,” Raeg replied, following.

The werewolf licked his lips. “Oh yeah... that's good,” he said. “Uh... I mean it's not even half of what I do in a usual day, but I had to baby you, give you the easy ones. It's slowed me down a lot.”

“That troll was easy?” Raeg asked, referring to the Crag troll from a few hours back. The thing had thrown him through the wall of a building and into a restaurant. Amazingly, Raeg had barely felt it and jumped right back up and beat the tar out of the thing. Yem had taken that tag also.

“Why are you holding all the tags?” Raeg said.

“Told you, scum. You're not rated for that yet,” Yem replied quickly. “You gotta earn it. Third class is nothing, worse than nothing. You're not fit to lick the shit from my shoes.”

The werewolf always had some snappy reply and it always included an insult.

“You don't wear shoes,” Raeg said. “You're a werewolf.”

“You know what I mean,” the creature replied.

They walked in silence then, heading toward the closest furnace. If Raeg was right, and he had been every time so far, all they had to do was continue down despair street until they came to Thenul boulevard. They took a left there and walked until they came to the furnace.

Unfortunately, the silence didn't last long.

"So you don't remember nuthin' from up top?" Yem asked.

"You mean..."

"Bein' alive, yeah. What, are you dumb?"

Raeg grit his teeth. "No," he said. "I don't. You said you'd teach me somethin' else, somethin' important."

"Yeah, that'll have to wait til' tomorrow," Yem replied, scratching at a balding spot on his fur. Several little black creatures leaped out. Raeg would have thought them fleas except they floated away instead of jumping.

That was good... he hated bugs. Though if it turned out Yem had bugs, that'd be ample reason to stomp him dead wouldn't it? It felt like it should be.

"I thought today was the only day of training," Raeg said. This wasn't strictly true. Vigolos hadn't said anything about tomorrow but as it stood, Raeg had done all the work while Yem watched and it hadn't even been that hard. The troll had been the worst one of the day but even he had gone down after only a few punches. Raeg hadn't even been forced to use the baton he'd been issued, not once. That was good though, the thing stunk like it had been rubbed in rot.

They arrived at the furnace soon enough. "Just wait a sec," Raeg said. "I'm comin' this time."

"No!" Yem snapped, a little too quickly. "I told you. You do the body, I do the tag. It's faster that way, and they only deal with people of my rank, you understand?"

"Oh I understand," Raeg said as he put the unconscious reaper on the ground in front of the furnace as it gaped in front of him like an open mouth, waiting to be fed. Then he waited a couple seconds and followed Yem.

Though he couldn't remember much from his past, something told him this guy was screwing him and if he just followed, he'd find out how.

"Another one already?" a high nasally voice asked. It was close enough for Raeg to pause and wait behind a corner.

"You know me," Yem replied. "I work hard."

Both voices broke into laughter.

"You better make sure that Barbarian doesn't figure out your skimming him," the high voice said, making a clucking noise.

"Keep your voice down moron!" Yem replied. "He's over burning the carcass. And NO, I don't worry about it. That human is dumber than a sack of wet rocks. Eventually he'll meet a loyalist strong enough to kill him and I'll laugh my hairy ass off."

"You gonna give him anything?" the other voice asked.

"Nah!"

They both laughed.

Raeg's fists clenched.

~

MAX HUNG on the bottom of the ladder, waiting. He wasn't a huge fan of heights. The good news was that there wasn't any water the thousand or so feet below him. The ocean was over to the ship's left, nice and distant. Out ahead, near where the pirates had landed, the Reylosian cutter was approaching. It was flying flags with stripes of orange and white just like the guards at that crappy town.

A little closer Mytten, he thought. Tell them to pull ahead about a hundred feet.

A few seconds passed and then Max felt the ship begin to move. He was the only part of it sticking out of the bottom of the thick gray clouds that hung over the city of Rey like a perpetual bad mood. Mytten was on the bridge. Though she had no voice box to relay his instructions, she could gesture and Trina would tell Tela and the ship would move.

How's that?

Good, he thought. The enemy ship was just about to slide into position beneath them. Just a little more and he would tell them to drop.

"Alright, here I go," Max said.

There was a hiss from his right shoulder. Max's head whipped around.

"Scruff! I told you to stay on the ship! I don't want you getting hurt!"

Scruff wrapped four of his tentacles together into a knot and shook.

Max sighed. "Well... I guess it's too late now. Just hold on tight," he said as he looked back down at the cutter.

He could see why the pirates wanted it. It was moving pretty fast, and it boasted a row of good sized weapons. As Max looked at it, he couldn't help but think of an old school masted ship... only covered with metal and propellers and without the masts and the sails. Yeah, it was completely different. But they both had guns, or at least, things that fired like guns.

"Ok Mytten, let's go," he said. There was a lag of a few seconds as the instructions were relayed and then The Midnight dropped from the clouds, heading straight down toward her prey below.

The wind was picking up a bit, which wasn't the best, but Max wasn't planning to drop too far. Once Tela was out of the clouds she'd be able to navigate on her own and adjust to put him dead in line with the enemy ship. Then he would drop on them from above, like a bone bomb.

Bite! Bite! Bite!

"I'm sure you will, Scruff," he said.

The cutter was still coming straight on, heading right for the landed pirate ship. It looked like they hadn't seen them, which was good because the only advantage they had on this bigger ship with more guns, was speed. If the enemy saw them and decided to bring their guns to bear, it could get ugly.

"This plan is nuts," Max said. He was almost there though. He could see the top hatch on the cutter. Tela was lining him right up with it. Just another hundred feet or so, then...

The cutter turned, hard.

"Shit!" Max said. There was no time to wait. "Hold on!" he warned Scuff and let go.

The wind rushed through his helmet, whistling and causing the visor to flap up and down twice in the few seconds it took for Max to slam into the top of the Reylosian cutter.

3 damage received.

He hit hard enough to bounce and almost flew off the side of the ship. He would have if the wind hadn't changed direction enough on his way down for one of the long flags that flew from the top of the ship to flick in his direction. It was close enough that he snatched at it with his right hand and managed to catch hold somehow.

The flag went taught and ended up being the only thing between him and a very long fall. Max then used it to drag himself back up to the top of the ship and rolled over a short railing before dropping onto his back with a relieved sigh.

He found himself staring up at one of the flags that had saved him, flying overhead. Didn't these people know anything about wind resistance? It seemed stupid to be flying such long flags on an attack ship. The flag itself was orange and white, but there was a crest on it too. A White field with a stylized representation of something. It was hard to make it out when it was moving.

Well... whatever.

He sat up, looking over to his right. Scruff was still there, clinging to his armor. The creature waved at him.

"Time to go to work," he said.

There was a banging from below him. When Max looked down, he saw that he was actually sitting on the hatch he was supposed to use to get in. People were banging on it from below. Max slid aside and used a gauntleted fist to bang back.

"Knock, knock," he said, flipping down his visor.

The hatch opened.

"What are you doing here?" snapped a Reylosian, his own helmet visor up. "You're supposed to be up there with them!"

This was news.

"Uh... I fell?" Max said.

The man frowned. "You idiot. Where's your griffin? Get in here!" Then the soldier's eyes widened. "Wait... What in Cerathia's name is that thing?"

Scruff hissed.

Max summoned his secondary weapon, the black iron axe and whacked the guy right in the top of his helmet. The soldier collapsed down into the ship.

"You blew my cover buddy," Max said.

Scruff shrugged.

"You should try to stay out of sight. In this armor I don't look like an enemy to them."

Max then slid feet first into the hatch, landing with a crash on top of the soldier he'd seen a second before who was crumpled at the bottom of the ladder. Two other Reylosian soldiers were nearby. Each held a short sword and a small shield, ideal for the cramped quarters of a ship corridor.

"Get him!" one yelled as they attacked.

7 damage received.

6 damage received.

8 damage received.

4 damage received.

Each of the enemies did two quick stabs as they moved to surround him. The good news was that though the corridor itself was tight, the area around the ladder was more open in a circle, probably to facilitate moving men and equipment up and down, maybe even for defense.

Whatever the reason, it was just wide enough for him to brandish both weapons and go on a spinning, hacking, slashing rampage. Six attacks in only a few seconds. Two of the axe attacks were blocked, but Max didn't really care. It was the drain sword that mattered.

32 health received.

36 health received.

30 health received.

"Ahhhhh," Max said. "That's the good stuff."

"You despicable fiend," another enemy said as the two soldiers Max had just diced dropped to the ground. He looked like the captain. "Stealing the life of my men with that profane weapon," he shook his head. "You will pay."

He wore expensive looking clothes with a long coat, a pointed hat and a thick scarf that wrapped around the lower half of his face. In his right hand he held a short sort of wooden cudgel. Max was immediately reminded of another airship captain from this world, back in Celain. That guy had been self assured too, but he'd been wearing a heck of a lot less.

"You're not a Monk," Max said.

The man laughed. It was a heartless empty sort of chuckle. "You're perceptive for a vile creature without the guts to show his face," he replied, the stern gaze of this cold yellow eyes overflowing with self-righteous anger. "Tell me, what sort of phohor are you under that helmet? Are you an orc, an imp, a dark elf?"

Max attacked immediately, swinging the black iron axe and sword as fast as he could, but his enemy deflected all but one of the attacks.

38 health received.

"That's a nasty bite you have," the captain said.

A flurry of attacks from the cudgel followed in quick succession. Max managed to deflect one of them, but the others clanged against his armor and helmet.

13 damage received.

13 damage received.

"Why do you care what I am?" Max replied, trying to understand why this guy was hitting him so easily. "I'm just some guy."

"Now that," his opponent said, "was a lie."

15

DOWN AND OUT AND UP AND AWAY

"How do you know that was a lie?" Max replied. What class was this guy?

The man smiled and smashed him two more times, easily bypassing Max's guard.

21 damage received.

23 damage received.

Dammit! Why were his attacks getting stronger?

Max responded with his own series of strikes, but every one of them either missed or was deflected. What the hell was going on?

"Your stench gives you away, undead," his opponent said with a twinkle in his eye. Then he held up his weapon. "Goddess grant me warrant to impose your will upon this undead." The man's cudgel began to glow with a bright yellow sheen as if someone had turned on the switch of a torch inside it. Little barbs and thorns began to force their way out of the wood.

"What the crap is that?" Max asked.

"Your doom, undead," he said. "I judge you guilty! You shall be destroyed!"

"Oh my god!" Max said. "Do you ever shut up?"

We have a problem up here.

It was Mytten. Max held up a hand to the captain, "Hold that thought chief, I've got a call."

"What is it Mytten?" he asked.

His enemy stared at him, looking shocked. "You... I'm sorry, what?"

You wanted us to move above the clouds after we dropped you.

"Yes," Max replied. "That's what I wanted."

There's another ship up here. A big one.

"Another ship?" Max blurted. "Where?"

"HA!" the captain said, pointing his glowing cudgel at Max's head. "We knew those pirates would return. Now you're all going to learn what happens to those who steal from Reylos!"

"If they didn't see you, hide in the clouds and don't come out," Max said. "If they did, run."

We're not leaving you.

"Yes you are," Max replied.

"Enough!" the captain said, raising his cudgel to strike. "Now we finish this."

Max looked at his enemy. Things weren't looking good for him here. Even if he could win this fight himself, it would take too long to do it. This guy wasn't a monk, he was some kind of combat class. His ability was glowing yellow. Yellow. "Hey, Scruff."

The tentacled crawler appeared from where he was hiding under Max's cape.

"Sic' em."

The captain's eyes went wide.

That was one thing Max remembered well about the affinities chart: decay beats commitment and few living creatures embodied the poisonous nature of decay more than his swamp loving dungeon crawler.

Scruff vaulted onto the man's face, wrapping his tentacles securely around the back of the man's head. Just the sight of it made Max wince but not enough to miss his chance to jam the drain sword deep into his enemy's chest over and over. The guy dropped his special glowing weapon and started desperately trying to pry Scruff from his face with his fingers but the creature had grown quite a bit and was far too strong.

38 health received.

31 health received.

39 health received.

33 health received.

36 health received.

32 health received.

Two more crew members appeared behind Max. They wore no armor and carried only short swords with no shields. Max rounded on them and pushed up his visor, revealing a bare black skull with glowing green eyes.

The men screamed and ran back the way they'd come.

Max laughed.

Behind him, with much of his head now devoured by Scruff, the captain finally slumped to the floor.

Reylosian regulars and Reylosian Inquisitor defeated!

You've gained a level of Mercenary!

"What?" Max said. "Nice!"

Inquisitor huh? Interesting.

There was no time to goggle over his new stats though, he had to get this ship down per the plan. Max marched toward the front of the ship. On his way he passed an open door where a crewman was quivering inside.

The man was a bit portly and wore a stained white apron over his crew uniform. He looked like a cook. Oddly enough the room he was in, which now that Max looked more closely, sure did look like a small galley, smelled pretty good. If it smelled good to an undead, that didn't bode well for the living crew.

Max leaned in enough so that the glow of his green eyes cast a sickly pallor over the cook's face and apron. "Tell me, human... which way to the bridge?"

The man pointed to Max's right with a single shaking finger, causing Max to notice half of the fingertips on the man's hand were missing.

"T... t... take the right ladder," the cook whispered.

Max nodded, "Thanks, carry on!"

Then he ran down the short corridor and turned right at its end. At the top of the ladder was indeed the bridge, a bigger one than the Midnight, with a better view. Two men were looking out above.

"Captain, the attack is going as planned, the knights have engaged both ships and-" one said until he turned around and saw Max. His jaw dropped. "Uh... I."

"Ship to the ground. Now," Max said but as he thought about it, maybe that wasn't the best idea. He had to find out what was going on. "Who is attacking the other ship? What knights?"

"I won't divulge that to some unholy abomination! Die!" the closer man said as a sword appeared in his hand and he lunged. Max parried the blow easily before jamming his drain sword in the other man's chest.

67 health received.

The man dropped to floor. The other one put both of his hands up. "They're griffin knights from the light carrier Gallant."

Max sighed, wiping the pinkish blood from his blade on the kilt-like thing that hung from the bottom of his scale mail. Griffin knights. Those sounded familiar.

Right! His father's paintings. Griffin riding knights were a popular subject in some of his father's well known works. Wait, hadn't he seen paintings like that somewhere else too? That school Trina took him to. Of course! How had he forgotten about that?

Whatever, he had to figure out how to get up there. If they were attacking the Midnight, there was no way Trina with the little Scruffs and still recovering Mytten could hold them off. Not that they couldn't fight, but none of them had an answer for thick armor.

"Take us down. fast," Max said.

The man frowned, turning back to his console.

"I said take this ship down, now!" Max said.

"I heard you," the man said. "But you're wasting your time. The knights will be here soon, and-"

There wasn't time for stupid crap like this. The guy was stalling. Max ripped him out of his seat, throwing him to the back of the bridge. Then he sat down in front of the control console. It seemed similar to that stupid flying truck he'd stolen before.

"Here we go," he said, yanking the controls.

Down they went. It was too fast, but Max didn't really care. He'd told the pirates he would get the ship they wanted down. Nobody said it had to be intact.

Luckily they weren't too high up. It wasn't long before the ship smashed into a building below. Max twisted the controls to the side, causing the cutter to spin out, dragging a huge rut into the dirt of an open storage area.

"You fool! You could have gotten us all killed!" the bridge officer shouted at him.

Max stood up as the ship shifted beneath them, rolling a bit to one side. "Don't care," he said.

"I can't afford a revival!" the man said. "I'm not from some rich family that can pay with favors... if I die, I go into debt forever!"

Max rounded on him as he made his way toward the bridge exit, pointing a gauntleted finger in the man's face. "Don't blame me for the system you live under! This bull crap is all the light's doing. And I'll tell you right now: If I have anything to say about it, it's all gonna end!" Max said. "Now get off this ship!"

"MYTTEN! How are you? Is everything Ok?" Max asked as he kicked the last of the Reylosians out of the cutter.

They're on the ship. The small crawlers are preparing to fight the intruders. The girl has laid traps, as have I.

"You can lay traps? Like what? Wait... Never mind that. Tell Trina to bring the ship down below the clouds. Do you know how many of them there are?" Max asked as he stepped out into the waning light. His eyes were improving rapidly as the sun descended toward the horizon.

I gestured to go down. I don't know if she understood.

Max stopped and looked up. Scores of griffins circled above, at least a dozen of them. Six were close, almost to the ground.

I hear them banging on the metal. I don't think we'll last long.

"I'm coming," he said, pulling his visor down.

A griffin swooped low, coming right for him. Max was struck again by how familiar it looked. Straight out of one of his dad's paintings. Even the lance was identical.

Hmmm. Didn't his dad once paint one of those shooting something?

Just as it occurred to him, the lance glowed and a ball of bright white fire erupted from it. Max dove to the right. Only his improved agility let him dodge the attack in time. When he looked back, sprawled across the dirt, a giant flaming pit had been carved in the ground.

Max rolled over and scrambled back to his feet. He didn't have much time.

"Hey!" he yelled at the griffin. It had already swooped by and was now banking back around for another pass. "Are you too much of a coward to fight me like a man?"

Max clanged his sword against the black iron axe three times in challenge. It wasn't the same as his old brawler skill, but hopefully this time it would... nope.

The griffin didn't slow down at all, instead it beat its wings, speeding ahead.

"There goes that idea," Max said as he tried to dive out of the way, but the lance adjusted perfectly, spearing him right through his midsection.

37 damage received.

"Actually... that's not as bad as I expected," he said, grunting as he stored the axe and used his left hand to pull himself closer to the knight as the griffin flew back into the sky, dragging him with it. The knight was well aware of his plan however and after they'd risen around three hundred feet, he let go of the weapon and Max plunged toward the ground. After several seconds of screaming he slammed into the dirt with a thud as the lance ripped itself from what would have been hits guts, if he had any.

67 damage received.

"Ow..." he said, rolling over. He had to get up quickly because...

CLANG! A sword hammered into the back of his helmet.

23 damage received.

Max rolled to the side and up on one knee, swinging the axe as hard as he could, not to attack anything, really, just keep the guy back. It didn't work. The knight, in his shining armor, deflected the axe with ease. He then switched to a two handed grip and jabbed his sword at Max's chest.

The high angle of the attack is probably the only thing that caused it to glance off the Sun steel scales of his armor, giving Max a second to slash with his drain sword, aiming for the knight's gauntleted wrist. The blow was deflected harmlessly by the knight's armor but was enough to make his enemy back off and allow him back to his feet.

The worst part was that a second knight had landed nearby and was already approaching, sword drawn.

They've broken in. Please come quickly.

Clang, clang, CLANG. The knights sword rang against Max's axe and sword, driving him back. Max wished for the backslap skill. He really missed that. Actually...

He had that new skill. What was it called again? Damn!

While he tried to remember, there was only one thing to do: all out reckless assault.

Max let loose, smashing his weapons into the enemy knight as fast and hard as he could. The first two hits were parried, but after that the knight wasn't quick enough and Max's weapons started hitting home. He slashed at his neck, arm, and chest and finishing with a solid axe to the side of the helmet.

23 health received.

21 health received.

19 health received.

The stolen health helped a lot. Especially when the second knight's blade slipped past his guard and drove into his chest.

53 damage received.

Max renewed his assault. Axe, sword, sword, axe, hammering and slashing and chopping. He was trying keep the pressure on to prevent them from surrounding him. The second knight was better than the first one, he parried more than half of the attacks that went his way and followed up with a vicious slash that clanged into the side of Max's helmet, almost knocking it free of his head.

Max grit his teeth, feeling rage rise inside him.

Rage! Of course... that new ability was Vengeance.

When the first knight came in for another attack Max started to back away like he was preparing to flee, then lunged forward, allowing his enemy to stab right through his chest before he brought his weapons together as hard as he could on the knight's helmet.

47 damage received.

24 health received.

Blood gushed from the holes of the knights visor and he dropped to the muddy ground, pulling his sword free of Max's chest as he fell.

The second knight let out a howl of rage as he renewed his attack and Max let him, falling into a defensive stance for the first time in a long time. He blocked two of the attacks but the remaining two hit hard.

57 damage received.

51 damage received.

That was just fine, he thought as he stood up and attacked the now panting knight. His first attack was a straight up miss, the second was a hit with the axe but it was third, a vicious backhanded axe strike, where Max used the skill.

Vengeance!

He felt power surge through his arm, swinging the axe with an incredible force that ripped right through the armor protecting the knight's neck and tore his head free from his body in a single horrific blow. Max stood over him, victorious, struck again by how familiar the armor was. The sharp beak-like helmet angled to deflect wind during flight, the pointed breastplate designed to deflect lances, he'd seen it all before.

Griffin Knights defeated!

Max took a second to pull a salve from his inventory and apply it, rubbing it on his skeletal face, which was currently the only part of his body he could get to.

Health restored.

It felt wrong to be killing Griffin Knights, profane somehow, but at this point, what choice did he have? "Well... that's war," he said, noticing a glint of gold around the decapitated knight's neck. Could it be?

Max knelt beside him and pulled on the golden chain. At the end was an amulet shaped like a shield with a flying griffin on it. Max was suddenly back in his childhood, sitting in bed, with his father telling the story of the young griffin knight and how he'd earned his wings. They'd given him an amulet called a pakheta and told him to call his griffin with the sacred words.

"Sorry about this," Max said, pulling the amulet from the dead knight's neck. "But I've got to try something."

Acquired: Pakheta amulet.

He stood and equipped the amulet, removing the dark seeking one. "Hami Udachaum!" Max yelled in the direction of the two griffins nearby. "We fly!" he said again, this time in English. His father had told him both. He'd made him repeat it so many times... Not that he hadn't wanted to. Max had spent most of his childhood pretending to ride a griffin and fight dark monsters.

To Max's utter astonishment, one of the griffins responded immediately, beating its wings to fly over and bend for Max to mount him.

"You've got to be shitting me," he said as he climbed aboard. There was a hook in the front of the saddle that probably connected to the knight's armor, keeping him tethered to his mount. Max's scale mail had no place to connect it. "Guess no barrel rolls for me," he added as he grabbed the reins. There was one other thing to say, something he'd said literally hundreds of times as a boy: "Udana!" and a sharp jerk, the creature's wings spread, and the griffin took to the sky.

16

A HUG AND A LAUGH

"You said do the job any way I want," Raeg said pointing at his own chest. "I wanted to punch him until he stopped breathing."

Vigolos leaned forward in his high-backed leather chair, putting one sharp elbow on his dark wooden desk while the other rubbed his temples. "People don't actually breathe here, so you would have been punching him forever."

Raeg grinned. "I know."

Vigolos shook his head, his expression unchanged from the stolid disgust that marked his features when Raeg had entered. "While I admire your mettle, I can't have you killing my employees. Even if he was worthless, he was loyal and that's what we care about here: loyalty."

Raeg crossed his arms. "He was stealing my food money. Nobody does that."

"Not my problem," Vigolos replied.

"I want it back," Raeg said. "When he can use his arms and legs again-"

Vigolos raised an arm. "I have a job for you. You do this right and you'll earn your way back into my good graces and a handsome payout as well."

Raeg raised a bushy eyebrow. "Sounds good."

The dark elf's eyes narrowed as he placed a piece of paper on the desk. Then he flicked a finger and the paper flew through the air toward Raeg, stopping in front of his face.

"A building east a here," Raeg said, frowning. "This has the address and everythin'."

"Is that a problem?" Vigolos asked.

"Uh... no, just kinda surprisin'," Raeg said. "Mostly the jobs just say a street or an area. They don't say the house."

"She's been there for months," Vigolos replied. "Those who've tried to bring her in, have failed."

"What do ya mean?" Raeg asked.

"They died. Still up for it?" the elf asked, clasping his hands together on his desk with the fingers interleaved. "The reward will be triple a normal job."

It sounded like a setup. That was just fine.

"Yep."

"Good," Vigolos replied as the paper hanging in the air suddenly caught fire and burned to ash. "Contract accepted. Prove your loyalty to the dark and your obedience to me, or its you who'll be hunted next. Now go."

Raeg grumbled to himself as he walked the dark streets of the city. Narak, they called it. Capitol of the underworld, once the center of the dark kingdom. The decaying remnants of the castle of death loomed over the city like a bad dream but you could still see it if you wanted to, all you had to do was find one of the streets that radiated out of the city center like spokes on a wheel. Raeg was passing one now but he didn't look.

He didn't care to.

The whole city was a slimy scum pit. From what he'd seen so far it was one big ugly slum full of swindlers, schemers, and bureaucrats. Maybe this was always how it was. Maybe the king just got fed up with it and that's why he left. Raeg could see that, actually. He was starting to feel that way himself.

He heard a noise to his right, like bones clicking.

"Hey Max, I had a funny thought..." he said, pausing in the street. Then he frowned. Max? Who was that?

A creature stood in the street nearby. He was stooped, wearing a shabby hooded robe. He took a step closer, using a cane which clacked against the ground.

"Raeg?" a soft throaty voice whispered.

Raeg grimaced. This looked like it might be that guy who'd called to him on his first day. He'd learned a few things since then. He had a job to do, and talking to people who inexplicably knew his name wasn't one of them. He started walking again.

"Don't go there," the voice called after him.

"Shut up," Raeg replied.

"They've sent you to die," the hooded man said.

Raeg stopped, looking back. "I'm already dead."

"You will be consumed and be no more. Don't go there, don't attack her."

"Who is she?" Raeg asked. If this guy knew something, it was probably worth it to find out. If he wouldn't talk. Raeg would make him.

"She's a dragon, or she was, once. She's angry and more powerful than you by far. Don't go. They've sent you to her to be rid of you. You probably did something they didn't like."

"Maybe," Raeg replied. No maybe about it, but the guy had it coming. He turned to leave.

"Don't go Raeg," the voice called. "There's a lot veiled from you here. Can you remember anything of your life before? Haven't you noticed that your interface is missing?"

"What? What does that even mean!" Raeg snarled.

"The dark needs you."

Raeg shook his head and continued on, cursing under his breath. "My hairy ass."

The man didn't call after him again and the walk was just as easy as he'd expected. In a short time Raeg arrived at what had once been a massive stone building. All that remained was a series of piles of rubble surrounded by the smashed remnants of a wall. The destruction wasn't natural either, not that anything in the land of the dead was natural, but purposeful. Each stone had been shattered. Few remained of any size bigger than a fist.

He didn't hesitate, he just walked right in and started climbing his way over the nearest pile toward the center.

"You're a brazen one," a woman's voice said.

Raeg looked around, but he couldn't see her. A dragon ought to be pretty easy to see.

"Another idiot sent to die by those betrayers?" she asked. "Come forth... and receive your compensation for this intrusion."

Finally Raeg managed to climb to the top of the first pile of rocks, giving him view into the rest of the rubble. There was a pile in the center slightly taller than the others. On its peak sat a long lithe woman with black hair and bright violet eyes.

"You aren't a dragon," he said.

"Disappointed?" she replied.

"Nah... It's all the same in the end," he said, sliding down the other side of the pile of shattered stone and patting one fist into the other. "Let's get this over with."

"Eager to embrace nothingness?" she asked, standing. The dim light of the underworld played across what looked like a cross between a small dress and dark steel scale mail.

"That thing you're wearing won't stop my fists."

She shrugged. "This is not really a dress. I'm not really a woman. And you... are not a man."

Raeg's lip curled. "Stop with the bullshit!" he barked and charged at her, swinging a solid right.

Deftly she ducked his blow, coming perfectly in line with his left jab, until... she wasn't. The punch didn't so much miss as it rubbed along her cheek. She spun, going with the fist, putting both hands on Raeg's left arm. Then she dropped.

The force was incredible. Raeg was thrown all the way across the ruined building and slammed into the side of one of the larger hills of broken stone. It hurt like hell.

Before he even had a chance to shake off the stun he heard thunderous footsteps pounding against the broken stone. A hand grabbed him by the back of the neck and threw him back, over the central pile of rubble, only to smash head first into another.

"Gah," he said, feeling his body. It ought to be broken by now, smashed to a bloody pulp, but there was no blood and no pain. All he felt was weakness, a kind of hurt in his core that drained him.

This time at least he was able to sit up and catch sight of her above him. She'd used the central heap as a ramp to launch herself into the air and was now coming down with a heel pointed right at his head. Racg dove to the side, barely making it out of the way.

She hit the stone with an uproarious crash, showering Raeg and everything around in bits of pulverized stone. So that was how this place had been trashed. It was her.

"You're not going to get away," she said. "I'm going to pound the power out of you and eat your soul."

Raeg laughed. "Sweetie, I thought you'd never ask."

Her eyes flared. "You! You disgusting human!" she shouted as she whirled around and grabbed him by the arm, swinging him up and then down to smash face first into the piled stone. "As if I'd ever sully myself!"

She grabbed him from the ground, raising him up over her head, preparing to bring him down over her knee or throw him, it didn't matter. He felt so weak now, he wasn't sure he'd survive another one.

He had to think of something. What was the worst possible thing?

"Hey! Watch it... there's... there's bug in your hair," he said.

He felt a tremor in her arms as a shiver ran down her spine. She shrieked and dropped him.

"No! No! No! Get it off! Get it away!" she screamed, turning in circles, flailing her arms and legs.

Raeg slowly returned to his feet. "Come here, I'll get it." he said, trying not to retch at the idea. There was nothing there. He made it up. Remember that. No bugs, not really.

She was crying now, sobbing, her hands over her eyes. "Please! Please! Please!" she begged. "Please..."

"I said GET OVER HERE!" he yelled.

She sniffled and obliged, still covering her eyes with her hands.

Raeg put a hand in her hair and pulled it away quickly, miming the act of removing something from her hair, just the act of pretending nearly made him gag.

"There," he said. "It's gone, dead."

"Throw it away!" she pleaded. "I don't want to see it!"

"You won't" he said. Because it doesn't exist. That didn't stop him from scratching at his neck though... The thought of something crawling on him. Ugh.

She sighed and fell to her knees, still sobbing.

Raeg stood over her. "You... ah... alright?"

She shook her head.

Raeg sat down next to her. "Come here," he said, opening his arms to the dragon woman who only moments ago had been trying to murder him.

Instead of becoming angry she nodded, sniffling and leaned in to put her head on his shoulder.

He wrapped his arms around her, holding her as she sobbed for some time after.

I know how you feel, he thought. I really do.

"What the dark is going on here?" said a female voice.

MAX GUIDED his griffin high into the sky, slipping right past the other knights. They didn't notice him. He had the right color armor, if not exactly the right kind and they had their sights below, probably on the pirates. More than one of those knights would be hard for them to handle but Caerd and his crew would have to fend for themselves. Max had other priorities.

It wasn't long before he saw it. Still painted in the muted blue of Kestria, the Gyre falcon patrol ship Tela had named Midnight was just below the edge of a thick patch of swirling gray clouds. Four Griffins flew in circles around it, not one had a rider.

Max stuck his gauntleted hand out ahead, pointing near his griffin's left eye.

"Jaggah!" he yelled. He still knew the command to land. So many times he had imagined this exact scenario as a boy. Riding a griffin into battle, clad in a knights shining armor. Only in those fantasies he hadn't been a skeleton. He'd always imagined fighting skeletons actually, using his sword to chop through undead hordes and goblins and orcs. Oh well. Times change.

His griffin climbed above the Midnight, dipping into the clouds for a second before diving down toward the top of the ship. The top hatch was open. The knights were already inside.

Max clenched his teeth as his mount closed in on the Midnight but then a hard gust of wind blew them off course flinging Max and his mount into the clouds. The creature spun, trying to right itself, forcing Max to hang on with all his might. The force was too much, despite his strength he was being torn from the animal like a doll from the back of a bounding dog.

It was at that moment, as he fought to retain his grip, that his griffin emerged again from the clouds. The carrier dominated the sky above him. It was a behemoth thing, easily as large as that ship of the line he'd seen back in Kestria, but flat, with gigantic maneuvering propellers that cut great circular holes in the clouds. It was only in seeing the size of the thing, that Max began to understand how thoroughly they'd been screwed by its arrival.

"Mytten!" Max yelled as his grip began to give out. "Move the ship, have Tela run!"

It's too late Max. The battle is joined here.

"Dammit!" he said as the griffin he rode was forced to swoop up and over the carrier, jerking Max free. He was flung through the air where he spun and tumbled onto the deck of the great flying ship. He landed with a clinking and scraping as his Sun steel armor dragged along the metal clad deck.

When he looked up, Max and found himself in the midst of five griffin knights preparing their mounts surrounded by their squires, attendants and various other ship personnel. A light drizzle had begun falling on the deck, coating the armor-clad knights and their griffins with a shimmering skin of reflective moisture. It was a surreal moment, straight out of one of his father's paintings. He couldn't help but stand there for a moment, struck dumb the the sight.

A knight approached. “Sir, are you well?”

Right... the armor. His helmet visor had clanged closed on impact. Like on the other ship, these guys were assuming he was an ally.

“I'm fine... uh... good sir,” Max replied. “Where might I find the captain? I must speak with him!”

The griffin knight clapped him on the shoulder with a shining white gauntlet. “Of course!” he turned to his right. “Kyne!”

A man wearing a dirty white tabard with the bright blue and red emblem of a griffin holding a sword in its beak, ran up. “Yessir!”

“Take this man to the captain,” the knight said.

“My thanks to you,” Max said as stuffily as he could and followed the other guy. He looked like he probably tended to the Griffins or something. The tabard was covered with stains from what looked like grease or maybe food and there was a little pouch at his waist that hung open and inside Max could see a bunch of fish.

So the griffins ate fish? Huh. You learn something new every day.

The wide open deck of the carrier was exactly what you'd expect: flat, with occasional hooks for griffins to be tied to, buckets of water, and lots of people, moving constantly as the knights prepared to take off or land. There wasn't a runway like on a carrier back home, but that made sense given the griffins had bird wings and could land relatively easily on their own in a short area. Two ramps ran along either side of the deck. They appeared to lead down into the ship, probably to griffin stalls, or something similar.

Maybe that was where they changed the oil, Max thought with a chuckle.

The guy Max was following was heading toward the right one. "Is it alright if we head down through the bay?" he asked.

Max nodded, "Uh... sure." That felt wrong though. Wouldn't the bridge be above, in that tower at the back of the airship? As he looked ahead, there appeared to be a group of armored men loitering around down there. That seemed odd.

Max stopped and looked back. Four Knights were walking in a line behind him, swords drawn.

They were on to him! The knights were trying to hem him in so he couldn't run for the edge of the ship.

"Well... shit," he said. What possible plan could there be in this situation but fight like hell?

He drew his sword and axe. He knew the knights were tough but the guys downstairs looked more like regular soldiers. It was time for a game strategy Max knew well: the little guys die first.

He turned on his heel and charged down the ramp.

Six soldiers appeared from all directions ahead and Max met them head on. The soldiers there were even easier to defeat than he expected, maybe level four or even five. He deflected their attacks and stabbed or chopped them one by one until they all lay on the ground before him, dead. He'd been hit a couple times but it didn't matter with the drain sword's healing.

Order of the Sky Sword foot soldiers defeated!

Order of the Sky Sword? Max had heard of that before... but when?

"Hey!" yelled a voice from behind him. The knights were still coming. They'd been forced to slow a bit on the ramp but were now picking up speed. Max took off running. He'd been hard pressed to beat two of them individually, but four at once? That could be a problem even with Scruff to help... wait.

He'd left Scruff behind in the other ship! Dammit! How could he do that?!

Max ducked into a doorway intending to slide down a ladder into the bowels of the carrier but instead strong fingers grabbed his armor from behind. Someone with incredible strength ripped him out of the doorway and threw him back into the center of the four knights.

"Stand away from him," said a voice, a young woman's voice... a familiar one.

Max turned around, struggling to his feet as he tried to take in what he was seeing.

"Hello Max," she said. "Or should I say... Boneknight?"

17

FALSE ENEMIES AND TRUE FRIENDS

It was that girl from Trina's school, Brenna, or Brianna, or something. Reflexively Max backed away from her, moving backward on all fours but one of the griffin knights put a hand on his shoulder to stop him.

"I said leave him be!" She shouted. The girl looked completely different from the last time Max saw her. She was now wearing an unfamiliar type of gear. Fantastic shining white armor pieces hung from studded leather that was all dyed a soft powder pink. The short cape that hung from one of her shoulders was also white with a single pink stripe.

"What the hell are you wearing?" Max asked, standing back up. "Is that the barbie armor set?"

"Ha!" she said, her face breaking into a wide grin, her eyes wild with delight. "Ha HA ha ha ha ha! I knew it! You ARE from our world!"

Max's jaw dropped, but he continued backing away, pushing past the knights, who made no move to stop him. He would do so as long as the girl would let him. What were the chances someone with armor like that was under level fifty? Probably poor, especially if she'd been brought here like he was.

It was odd too because his eyes seemed to be seeing something behind her, hovering over her shoulder. It wasn't clear what it was but it had a vague sort of rainbow outline to it.

"I don't want to have to kill you," she said. "That doesn't have to happen. Tell me... When did you come from?"

Max took another step back. "What do you mean when? The year?"

"Yes! Yes! What year were you taken?" she asked, grinning widely.

Should he tell her?

"My name's Brittney, by the way. These people always mispronounce it as BrittNAY, like a bunch of idiots! After a while I just let them call me Brenna or Breylana."

Max chuckled a little. "Brittney? Were you... uh... an exotic dancer or something?"

She scowled at him. "What are you talking about? Are you seriously asking me if I was a stripper???"

Max backed off again. He'd made it out of the ramp area, the side of the ship wasn't too far behind.

"Just forget I mentioned it," he replied. "I'm from twenty nineteen."

Her eyes narrowed. "You're a baby then," she said and laughed. "I was taken from from nineteen ninety three."

"How old were you?" Max asked.

"Eighteen," she said. "And I still look the same as the day I arrived... only now I'm a lot older. It's literally every girl's dream."

"Yeah look at you... eighteen forever and I'm this..." he said, pulling up the front of his visor to reveal his blackened skull and glowing green eyes.

The griffin knights nearby gasped. Several of them whispered things to each other. Max was sure he heard 'unholy' and 'abomination' among other things.

"That's because you were called by the bad guys Max," she said.

Max backed away another few steps. Something about this girl just didn't feel right. "What do you mean the bad guys?" Max asked. "I mean, sure there are orcs and goblins and vampires and werewolves on this side, but I don't know if you've seen how those guys live. It's not that great."

"There's a reason for that, Max!" Brittney said, gesturing with her arms open. "I worked hard to make it that way."

"You did this?" Max asked. "You setup this tyrannical regime?"

Brittney laughed. "Tyranny? As if! Have you been to the floating cities in the core kingdoms? Have you seen the palaces, the glorious waterfalls, the super sexy men, and women too, I guess," she said, eyes to the side. "This place is a paradise, precisely because we purge the dark. We keep them down on purpose. They aren't good citizens Max, they don't obey, they don't join the church and worship like regular people. They steal and they destroy."

Max shook his head, stepping closer to the edge. "No... you're wrong."

"I'm not," she said. "I've seen it thousands of times. Do you think others haven't tried? There have been schools for them, cities for them, all kinds of stupid crap. But it all ends the same way: murder and mayhem. It's only a matter of time before the dark go berserk. They just don't live in civilizations. They aren't civilized Max and they can't be. Stop wasting your time with them."

Max shook his head. "No... I've seen their kindness. They deserve to live every bit as much as these people."

"Dude... are you serious?" Brittney replied. "No they don't!" A dagger appeared in her hand. With a motion faster than Max could even see, she whipped it at him. It pierced his scale mail, lodging in his chest to the hilt.

233 damage received.

"Augh!" Max said, falling to one knee. The dagger was burning. He stored the black iron axe and pulled it out of his chest, staggering as he stood back up.

Acquired Exalted Dagger of purity, Damage 57, durability 90/90, damage is purity.

1 damage received.

"Ah!" Max said as the dagger burned his hand through the glove. Some how he'd been allowed to equip the dagger, even though he was an undead... and it was burning him while glowing a pale blue.

"See?" Brittney replied. "That's a purity dagger. You're impure, tainted by the dark. But I can fix you. You can be human again if you join us. We can talk about movies and TV. This place is boring sometimes. I miss having someone from Earth to talk to."

"No!" Max snarled, slashing at her with his drain sword, as he did his left hand squeezed the dagger inadvertently, causing a cascade of damage notifications to appear.

1 damage received.

1 damage received.

1 damage received.

1 damage received.

1 damage received.

1 damage received.

1 damage received.

1 damage received.

All three times Max tried to attack her, Brittney deflected the blade, with just the one dagger in her left hand.

"You're not going to hit me Max," she said. "This class is called Bright Blade, it's a prestige class. I had to go through things you wouldn't believe to get it, but it was worth it, believe me. You don't even have a chance. I bet you don't even have any class upgrades. Not only that, but I'm level ninety-nine and I have been since I got here. The numbers on my little thingy are so high, I don't even remember what they are."

Max slashed at her again and again and again. This time one of them connected, a vicious slash to her thigh.

28 health received.

"Ha!" she said, laughing. "I guess I stand corrected, huh? Hella good job there." she laughed again.

Max had tried not to tighten his grip on the dagger, but it was hard not to while attacking so hard with his other weapon, and another cascade of messages followed.

1 damage received.

1 damage received.

1 damage received.

1 damage received.

1 damage received.

"What even is that class you're using? Mercenary? Have you even made it to level twenty five? What a loser!"

"Hey!" Max snapped. "I've worked hard for every damned point I've got."

"If you were on the light... I could get you to level ninety-nine in a day, in an hour," she said.

"That's... that's impossible," he said.

Brittney grinned. "Don't get all butthurt about workin' so hard for nuthin'" she said.

He looked behind him to the edge. The drop was at least eight hundred feet. He would die. Then she would just scoop him up anyway and do whatever she wanted.

"Think about it. You could have seven thousand health, just like me."

Max paused. "Wait, seven thousand? Seriously?"

Brittney's self-satisfied grin widened to the point where it looked like it might cut her head in half. "I know! It's probably too much for your little pea size brain. Actually, do you even have a brain in-"

"That's nothing!" Max said.

She frowned. "What?"

"You majorly screwed up," Max said. "At level ninety-nine you ought to have much more health than that. Tells me you don't understand this place as much as you think you do."

Brittney's lip curled into a vicious sneer. She looked like she was about to reply when her eyes widened, focusing behind him as she took a big step back. "Whoa," she said.

Max turned around. "Oh," he said.

ANOTHER EXPLOSION SHOOK the entire ship. Trina ran to a view port so she could see. Ah! There it was: a knight flying through the air like shiny, ugly, bird. He was even flapping his arms like wings as he plummeted toward the ground. Trina wasn't a trap master like a Trapper, or an expert on bombs like an Alchemist, but she'd picked up a few things. Explosive powders could do many interesting things when properly applied.

"Yeah!" she said. "That's one for me. What about the boys?" she asked, looking up at the giant spider situated on the ceiling above. Mytten put two of her front legs next to her head like she was sleeping.

"Ah.. got it," Trina said.

Max's little dungeon crawlers were pretty efficient in their own right. Poison and paralysis together were a winning combination. One bite had a good chance, but there were four of them, so if they got the drop on one of those knights, he was done for. She'd hoped they could handle at least one of the four boarders, and it seemed like they had. "Where are the other knights?"

Mytten shrugged.

"You set webs all over the ship!" Trina said. She couldn't even leave the bridge without getting stuck. "Can't you feel them moving around?"

The spider mimed chopping something.

Ah, right. It would make sense for the knights to go chopping through the webs. If that was the case they might make it to the bridge. The pirates had already destroyed the door so it wasn't possible to keep them out. It was time for her last resort. She looked up.

"Mytten, my little knife won't pierce their armor. If they get here I'm going to use a powerful paralysis poison gas. The closed in space will probably be too much for this old mask," she said. "It shouldn't affect you. Just... be careful."

The spider nodded.

"They're here!" yelled a voice. "I hear talking."

Trina pulled her mask down over her face. "Stay back!" she yelled. "I'll crash the ship if you take even one more step!"

"Go right ahead," the lead knight replied, his shining Suns steel armor was overlaid with brilliant markings of blue and red and the emblem of a griffin with a sword in its beak. "You'll be the one to die. Our order will simply revive us and you'll have accomplished nothing. Why not give up instead?"

Why did they always sound so insufferably smug?

Another knight was moving in behind him in the corridor still cutting at webbing there.

Trina pulled her knife and held it out. "Stay back!"

"Girl, stop this!" the knight said. "I despise unnecessary killing."

Trina laughed, bitterly. "Sure you do," she said, pulling the large vial from behind her back.

"Now... don't do anything rash!" he said.

Trina smiled as she smashed the vial on the floor.

A thick cloud of noxious black smoke filled the bridge in seconds, obscuring everything and flowing into the corridor. Trina dropped to the floor, hoping to crawl out under the majority of it before it got... to... her.

The first knight was coughing and stumbling, then there was a thump as he fell.

"Where do you think you're going you little swindler?" the other knight asked as she appeared from the smoke like an apparition.

Trina looked up, the knight's visor was open showing a woman. Despite the thick cloud of gas she seemed to be breathing without any trouble.

"But... how?" Trina asked. Her limbs were stiffening quickly. In only a few moments she wouldn't be able to move at all.

The woman knight laughed. "Oh you mean the poison gas you made? Why aren't I affected?" She held up her left hand where on the outside of the gauntlet there was a ring with a single blue stone. "Poison immunity my dear," she said with a sneer. "It was a gift from my grandfather. I'd share it with you but I'm afraid it only works for the pure of heart."

Mytten slammed into the knight from behind, using her full weight to bowl the woman over before quickly jabbing fangs into the back of her neck. Mytten then started pulling thread to spin the woman up but a silver sword flashed, clipping the end from one of Mytten's legs.

The spider squealed and hissed with fury.

"Foul beast!" the knight roared as she scrambled away, slashing with her sword. "How dare you bite me!"

Mytten turned ever-so slightly toward Trina and then back to the knight. Trina knew, she knew how the spider must be feeling.

"She's... immune... poison," Trina said. Every word was an incredible struggle, but her hands were even worse. They fumbled in her pouch, looking for an antidote... Oh... right. Those were in the inventory!

Having regained her footing, the knight went on the attack. She held a silver arming sword in her right hand and a long dirk in the other and she used them both with deadly efficiency. Mytten tried to back off, but she was too large and there was little room to move inside the ship. Even if the spider vaulted to the ceiling, the knight was tall enough that she would be well within range.

Trina summoned a paralysis antidote and poured it into her mouth as quickly as she could, hearing a thud as another leg was cut from Mytten and the spider fell. Black blood gushed out onto the deck and the knight's shining white blade.

"You... stay... away... from... her!" Trina snarled. Then she had an idea. "Tela, roll the ship! Now!"

"Wow? Really?" Tela asked.

"Yes, really!" Trina screamed.

"You bet!" Tela replied and everything spun in a great circle around them. Trina and the knight and Mytten were all tossed around like nuts in a cup. The knight was wearing that heavy plate armor though, so when she hit a corner and then a solid wooden spar, the force was multiplied. The impacts were more than enough to knock the wind right out of her.

"Sorry about this," Trina said as she pulled her knife. "I may be a doctor, but sometimes I do harm." Then she stabbed the knife into the knight's neck, multiple times. As many as were necessary.

Notifications scrolled by on her arm, notifying her of a skill up, a level up, and something else, something incredible.

"Mytten? How are you?" Trina asked.

The spider, looked terrible, three of her front legs were more than half gone from the knight's vicious attacks. Trina paused to rub some salve on her quickly.

"Is that enough?" Tela asked happily. "Would you like to do another?"

"No!" Trina said as she quickly wrapped bandages around the poor spider's limbs to stop the bleeding. Mytten would be fine. It ought to be about time for her molt anyway. When that happened, the spider would be like new, if they could get her enough food.

"I'll be back," Trina said, heading back to the bridge. "Where are we?" she asked, looking out the front view port. Then she took off her mask. "Is that... Is that Max? And Brenna! Or Britnay... or whatever her name is!"

Trina couldn't see much of the situation but it didn't look good. Max was surrounded by four griffin knights with Brenna at their center. They'd backed him up to the edge of the ship. Trina would have to do something about that.

"Tela," she said. "Ramming speed."

18

VENGEANCE IS SWEET AND CUDDLY

The Midnight ploughed into the upper left side of the much larger carrier. Her bow seemed well enough designed for the maneuver, though, because it ripped a neat triangular wedge into the carrier's upper deck, like a knife cutting a cake. Then it dragged along the top deck, scraping wooden deck boards and metal plating up as it went, before coming free on the far side, seemingly unscathed by the impact.

Max, Brittney, and the four knights all dove out of the way, each heading in their own direction. When the Midnight had finally pulled free of the carrier, Max found he was still near Brittney and two of the knights.

"Who the hell is piloting that thing?!" Brittney asked. "A crazy person?!"

Max dragged himself to his feet. "Trina probably," he replied.

"That girl isn't just a weirdo nerd, she's a certifiable nutcase!"

Max shrugged. "No. She's my friend."

"You choose the wrong friends Max. You have a real problem with that," she said.

"I think I'm just fine," he replied.

1 damage received.

Dammit, that stupid dagger was still damaging him... Wait.

Wait, Wait, Wait! Yes!

Would it work? He'd have to be careful. Max needed to keep her talking and maybe whittle her down a little. He pointed to Brittney's left. "Whoa... is that Joey from friends?"

"What? Where!?" she said, her eyes widening.

Max attacked, slashing her twice with his sword and once with the dagger. While her guard was down, all three hits connected.

19 health received.

23 health received.

And he made sure to squeeze the dagger as hard as he could.

1 damage received.

1 damage received.

1 damage received.

1 damage received.

1 damage received.

1 damage received.

1 damage received.

1 damage received.

1 damage received.

1 damage received.

1 damage received.

1 damage received.

1 damage received.

1 damage received.

"Ha HA!" Brittney said, grinning, her eyes even wider. "That was a good one! I haven't heard anything about Friends in over six hundred years!"

"I knew you'd be a Joey girl," Max said, wondering why the same stupid: look at that trick kept working in this world. Was everyone an idiot?

"What? But you weren't even born when I was watching it. How do you even know about that show? Is it still on in twenty nineteen?" she asked.

"Actually, my dad told me about it a long time ago" Max replied, pausing his attacks for a second. "He said women can be categorized by which guy from the show they like, with those who like Joey being the dumbest."

"WHAAAAT?" Brittney shrieked. Another dagger appeared in her hand to join the first. "That's so MEAN! Oh... Don't tell me what to do!"

She seemed to be talking to someone behind her shoulder.

"Who's your friend?" Max asked, squeezing the burning blue dagger again.

1 damage received.

1 damage received.

1 damage received.

1 damage received.

1 damage received.

1 damage received.

1 damage received.

1 damage received.

1 damage received.

1 damage received.

1 damage received.

The notifications were completely clogging his screen now. Was there a cap on the Vengeance skill? He sure as hell hoped not. At this point, it was his only chance.

"You could say she's my guardian angel," Brittney said, with an evil smile. "She says I should stop trying to sway you and just kill you."

"Good luck," Max said, squeezing the dagger and feeling the burn as more and more notifications filled the screen.

"Look, Max, I know where you're going and I know who you're going for," Brittney said. "Don't. Arinna is a conniving murdering monster. She's killed millions of innocent people. If I let you leave, if you were to let her out of her confinement, she would wreak havoc. She would destroy everything and everyone she could. I've been sent here to make sure that doesn't, Max... Boneknight," she shook her head. "Seriously, last chance. Join me, become a man again, live on right side, be good... Or I'm going to have to kill you."

Max thought of everything he'd been through in this world. The sadism of Tesh, the betrayals, the disgusting bigotry and gross oppression not just of the dark, but of everyone. He shook his head.

"No," he said and attacked.

She stood there and laughed maniacally as he attacked over and over again. Every hit was deflected or an outright miss. No healing and no damage. He couldn't even get her to take a step back. She just kept standing there looking bored, like he was just wasting her time.

"I'm going to tell you a secret," she said, still giggling. "Vita's wanted me to kill you ever since she heard you existed. She said you'd refuse to join us, that I'd be forced to kill you, but I wanted to give you a chance... I really did. This place gets so boring Max, seriously, but right now, you can't even touch me. I'm starting to think you aren't even worth my time."

He had to do something. Vengeance would only work if he could actually hit her. If she deflected the attack, all that damage would be wasted. Time for plan B.

"Big talk from somebody with a seventy plus level advantage," Max said. "I can't even hit you with those super daggers you have. You're just a coward hiding behind her equipment."

Brittney scowled at him. "Hey! You're wrong, you know! You think I need these? Here!" She threw them to the ground.

Max smiled. His attacks were immediate. She blocked the first, the second, and the third. Only when he was sure the fourth attack was about to hit... did he call it out in his mind.

VENGEANCE!

The attack was devastating. His saber-like drain sword came in at the perfect angle, slashing down on her left shoulder. It cut right through the pink armor, through Brittney's ribs and guts and spine in one great cleaving blow. Bright white blood gushed from her body as her top half slid off and her lower half wavered and fell. Oddly, her face held no malice, no contempt... only a look of genuine, heartfelt surprise.

7399 health received.

"Holy shit," Max said softly. He looked down to see the drain sword literally disintegrating into dust in his hands. The attack must have used up all its durability. Easy come, easy go.

The two griffin knights stood there, staring at him.

"Well?" Max asked them, looking from one to the other. "Who wants next?"

They looked at each other and ran.

"Heh," Max said, shaking his head. "Honor code my ass."

You've defeated Light Warrior Brittney!

You've gained a level of Mercenary!

You've gained a level!

You've gained a level!

You've gained a level!

You've gained a level!

You've gained a level!

You've gained a level!

You've gained a level!

You've learned: One with the Void.

Acquired: Skull of Akran Tayne.

"Seven levels!?!" Max exclaimed as he brought up the status screen.

Status	Boneknight	Betrothed	
Level	27	Mercenary Skill	45
Health	950/950		
Magic	1/1	Affinity	Dark
Skills		Magic	
Rekindle, Vengeance		Dead Weight, Teeth of Fate, Void Crush, Flame, Chill...	
Strength	35	Attacks x 2	37
Agility	15	Accuracy	85%
		Defense	75
Vitality	34	Evasion	8%
Mind	20	Magic Defense	12
		Magic Evasion	9%

Oh the health! It was so beautiful and it came with a shiny new spell to boot! And what was that item? Was it an unlock for a new class upgrade? With a skull, it had to be something good.

Then he looked down at the ground, at Brittney's bloody corpse. Silvery white blood. It was creepy seeing that coming out of a person. Would she have anything on her? She'd been alive for hundreds of years, she had to, unless she was wearing one of those cache amulets.

He leaned in and touched her foot. Nothing happened. Wait... What was that behind her corpse there? Max walked around her. There was something! Two somethings actually, wedged behind the girl's back. Max used his boot to slide her out of the way.

"Oh... another dagger," he said, but as soon as he touched it, the blade lengthened into a full size sword, actually bigger than full size, this thing was huge! It had a wicked set of serrations on it too, like it was made not to just damage, but to shred. Nasty.

Acquired Flesh Ripper Great-sword, Damage 137, durability 323/666, ignores 6 DR, 33% chance to inflict bled status.

"Oh baby!" Max said. "Come to papa!"

The thing was triple the damage of his next best weapon. Triple! He'd probably have to use both hands to wield it... but who cares? Flesh ripper!

There was still the other item to look into. It looked like a tiny box covered in chains. Max picked it up. "Oh my God... is this a loot box?!" he asked as he stored the item in his inventory.

"Your god can't save you," said a soft feminine voice. "She doesn't even know who she is."

MAX LOOKED up from his screen to see that shimmer he'd noticed before resolving into what he assumed was an angel but not like he might have imagined. It had white feathered wings, sure, but what was in the middle of them was most definitely not the tall slender woman he'd expected when Brittney had said: "Vita." What was currently floating, flapping, in front of him could only be described as a cross between a kitten and a welsh corgi.

"Are you... are you Vish's counterpart?" Max asked.

She folded her tiny arms. "I, Vittella Halka Enjiv, servant of the Divine Empress Cerathia, shall now smite you in the name of my lady."

Max looked behind him. The edge of the carrier ship was right there. Could he jump? Would it be worth it? Where was the damned Midnight? It had slammed into the carrier, dug a huge scrape into the deck and disappeared into the clouds. Maybe they'd finally listened to him and left. Even as he though that, he realized how unlikely it was.

"Don't waste your time," she said. "I just wanted you to know who was responsible for your purging. That way when you get back to where you came from you'll remember me and the light, and know that the Goddess Cerathia is-"

Max held up a hand. "One sec' here. Are you saying that if I'd been purged... I would have just gone back to Earth?"

The flapping fluffy thing paused for a second before replying. "Uh... right. Absolutely. So if that's what you want, why not just make it easy and hold still while I cast this spell?"

"I'm not sure I believe you now," Max replied.

"Well it doesn't matter," she said. "I'm going to do it either way."

Max leaned in. "Has anyone told you you're adorable?" he asked, reaching out to scratch the floating creature behind her left ear.

"Ohh! No! Don't do thaaaaaat!" she said as she leaned into the scratches.

It really was just a goddamned flying cat puppy.

"What did you mean that Arinna doesn't know who she is?" Max asked, still scratching.

"Under the chin... Ahhhhh," Vita said. "You'd find out... if I was going to let you live... but Ahhhhhhh... since I'm not."

"I think," Max said, looking up as something emerged from the clouds above. "That we'll meet again and I hope you... will remember these scritches and scratches you got..."

"Ahhhhhhh," Vita said. "Hmmm?"

The rope ladder was down and heading right for him. All he had to do was reach up and grab it. He was pulled into the sky away from a very startled little angel thingy. Max blew her a kiss and climbed the ladder.

Unfortunately he realized a bit too late that he'd left Brittney's two other daggers stuck into the ground where she'd thrown them. Oh well... at least he had the Flesh Ripper!

Inside, the scruffs were waiting for him. All four of them were jumping up and down, though a couple were missing some tentacles. But where was the big one...

Oh! Scruff!

"Trina!" Max yelled as he pulled up the ladder and closed the hatch. "Can you hear me?"

"Don't shout!" she replied, her voice echoing through the corridor. "Mytten is hurt and sleeping."

Again? Poor Mytten! Max quickly jogged down the hall, passing the remains of quite a few thick spider webs. On the way he saw Mytten, wrapped in a blanket in her room, black blood stained the bandages that wrapped the ends of her front legs.

Max cursed. Those damned knights.

Trina was on the bridge waiting for him.

"Tela said you'd know what to do," Trina said, smiling. "I was skeptical."

"Will Mytten be Ok? How did you handle all those knights? How's the Midnight?" he asked in quick-fire fashion.

"One thing at a time!" Trina snapped back. "Mytten will be fine, she just needs to sleep. We'll feed her and she should molt, then everything will be good as new. The knights... poorly, to be honest, but we did it. The ship has a few holes, and a lot of webs, but it's otherwise in good shape, right Tela?"

"You bet!"

"Can we not go ramming ships twenty times our size?" Max asked, taking a bridge seat across from Trina. Even as he said it he felt a little bad about it. The truth was that he'd come to rely on her. Trina wasn't just a supporting member of the party, she was a real asset, and a good friend.

"That was not my idea!" Tela said.

"Hush," Trina said. Then she looked at Max. "What can I say? I... didn't know what else to do. Did it help?"

"A little," Max said. He should tell her how much he appreciated her, how amazing it had been to look up and see that ladder hanging there... but... that was difficult. It just didn't want to come out. "What's the situation?" he asked instead.

"The griffin knights were mostly going down to stop the pirates, until you went up, then it looked like they were all called back. Now I don't know. They don't seem to be able to land on us while we're in the clouds," Trina said.

"What about the pirates?" Max asked.

"I happened to catch a glimpse of them when we zipped by that carrier," she said. "The cutter is up and away. They didn't even chase them."

"Alright," Max said. "What about Scruff? I left him on the Cutter by mistake. Did you see him down there?"

"No," She said. "Should we go down and look?"

Max grit his teeth. With all those griffin knights it would be a risk to check. Wait... there was an easy answer.

"One second," he said as he stepped out of the bridge and unequipped his armor before selecting Breeder from the class selection screen. He should be able to hear Scruff in his mind again.

Scruff? Are you there?

Max! Here! Here!

Where are you buddy? On the ground?

In ship. Hide. Pirates here. Bite?

No bite. Go with them and stay hidden, we'll meet you in a few hours.

Yes. Meet.

Max equipped his black leather and returned to the bridge. "He's with the pirates. We're done here. Full steam to the rendezvous!"

"Huh?" Trina said. "Did you mean full speed?"

"Number one, engage!" Max said. "Full throttle... warp speed... hyperspace calculations complete..."

"Ok! I get it! You're just saying nonsense to annoy me now," Trina said, grimacing. "Tela, let's go to the meeting place, as fast as you can, but stay in the clouds for as long as possible."

"Absolutely!" Tela replied. "It'll be a little shaky in here from the wind, is that alright?"

"Yes Tela," Max said. "That's just fine."

The Midnight clattered and banged as they swung around, using the clouds to head south toward the low line of peaks that marked the western end of the Valcas Mountains. The peaks even seemed to continue out into the sea as a line of islands jutted from the ocean waves like traffic cones. Mist swirled in the from the ocean, covering the valleys that wound inland with a thick white blanket. Tela descended right into the thick of it, shrouding their ship and obscuring it from prying eyes.

Max took the time while they cruised to check out his new item: The skull of Akran Tayne. It just sounded cool. Max hovered over the description.

The severed skull of the greatest general of King Gazric's elite Legion of Death, the most powerful and storied unit of his land forces. The skull is slightly blackened with soot and smells faintly of brimstone.

This was a key item as well, listed at the bottom in the exact same spot the gladius had been. There was no getting around it, this had to be a class upgrade. It also meant it would probably be a test. He liked it better when they just unlocked. What horrible things would be be asked to do in order to prove his worth for this one?

It was tempting to try it right away, but he wanted to be mentally ready and it wouldn't help to have another new class, once again at level one, even if it had great potential. Maybe he'd try for it on the way across the ocean, maybe.

"I think, this is it," Trina said, pointing ahead.

The meeting place was a second mountain hideout. It had been a little harder to find in the mist but they'd finally managed it. The cutter was already landed and offloading dozens of drums of fuel, ten of the circular containers had been separated off from the others.

"Do you think that'll be enough?" Max asked as the Midnight touched down on the flat stone, actually landing for the first time in at least a day.

Trina shrugged. "The pirates would know better than I would."

"Alright," Max said. "Let's go see Caerd."

Trina's eyes bugged. "Ah... yes."

19

A CLOCKWORK COMPANION AND A REBEL YELL

Caerd was waiting for them along with Shaena and three other pirates, including the one with the spectacles. As they approached, Max looked over at Trina, who'd put her mask back on. Quietly, he slipped into the equipment menu and unequipped it from her.

"Hey!" she snapped, reddening when she saw Caerd right in front of her.

"Max! Welcome back! I can't believe it, but you did exactly as you promised," he raised an eyebrow. "Though I will say the cutter took a bit of a beating when you drove it into the ground."

Max shrugged. "The pilot was an asshole. I did the best I could."

"It's fixable!" Shaena said. "Not an issue."

"I'm glad," Max said.

Then from Max's right, Scruff dropped out of a bent section of metal on the cutter's hull, flopping to the ground with a splat.

"Scruff!"

Max! Bite pirates now?

No buddy, they seem Ok, he thought.

Shaena looked ill. "That thing was on our ship? Again?!"

Max shrugged, bending down to pick up his friend who happily crawled back to his shoulder. "By the way... Caerd, have you met my comrade in arms here? Her name is Trina Bill, she's an excellent doctor, very knowledgeable."

Trina glared daggers at him.

"Ah... no I haven't," Caerd extended a hand, palm up for the dark style of handshake but Trina just stood there, staring at him.

"Shake his hand Trina," Max said, elbowing her.

"Uh... heh..." Trina said, weakly extending her hand for the ritual.

"She's... very good at treating minor injuries, things that plague you... you should really have a check up Caerd," Max said.

Trina was clenching her jaw with embarrassment now, it was kind of funny.

"Oh really?" Shaena said. "I have this bunion, and-"

"Anyway!" Max said. "Are those our fuel containers?"

"They are!" Caerd said. "All yours... and something else!" he turned to reveal a rusty metal contraption in the shape of a tall, thin cylinder.

The pirate with the spectacles put his hand on top. "Zaluur Basdog." he said.

Max recognized the high demonic immediately. The pirate had said: 'Navigator Arise.' No sooner had the words been spoken than a pair of arms and legs popped out of the cylinder, followed by a head and two bat-like metal wings.

"What is that?" he asked.

"Fascinating!" Trina said, for the moment enthralled by something other than Caerd's muscular physique and chiseled features. "That's an ancient demonic automaton! I read they were made for the Dark king by the Uhkaan Tentsuu. I've only seen them in museums and then only in pieces. It's got to be over a thousand years old."

"Spoils of one of our more interesting thefts," Caerd said, eyeing the metal creature. "It responds to questions in most languages but only replies in demonic. And it always knows how to get anywhere. The thing has a map of the world stuffed inside it, or so it would seem."

"One ugly ass smartphone wannabe if you ask me," Max said. "This is what you're sending to help us get across the ocean?"

"Yes," Caerd said. "But not to keep. You're borrowing it and Dag," he indicated the pirate with the spectacles. "Do whatever you need to over there and bring them both back."

Max crossed his arms. So a robot navigator huh? But does it speak bocce? "What's its name?"

"It responds to Korin," said Dag, putting his fingers through his long hair. "That's-"

"The number twenty," Max said. "If you only have to come to speak the high demonic, don't. I can handle that myself."

Caerd's eyebrows rose and he exchanged a glance with Dag who appeared to be relieved. "Full of surprises aren't you," Caerd said. "Though I suppose I shouldn't be. One minute a mage, the next a Mercenary who can take down trained griffin knights. I don't know what you are, but I'm pleased we could do business together."

"Yeah," Max said, though Caerd didn't actually look pleased, he looked unsettled. That was fine, though. Max felt the same unease about working with the pirates. The sooner they parted company, the better. "We ought to be going," Max added. "Come on Korin, board that ship right there."

"Tiim ezen," the creature said in a choppy metallic voice. It meant: 'Yes, lord.' It was a polite robot, apparently.

"You too Trina," Max said.

"Uh... right," she replied.

Max loaded the fuel containers aboard the Midnight, checking each one to be sure it was full of... something. He actually wasn't sure what was supposed to be in there but it felt like a good idea to check if it was just water or something. Not that he didn't trust the pirates... No... that's exactly why. He absolutely didn't trust them.

"Let's keep an eye on that navigator thing," Max said to Trina after he'd winched the cargo door closed and returned to the bridge. "Actually, where the hell is it?"

"It was buzzing around here, then it said something I couldn't understand and left," Trina replied.

"Shit," he remarked. "You stay here, I'll find it."

It took some searching but he found it cruising around the lower deck. The thing appeared to be going from room to room, like it was making a map of the ship or something.

"Hey!" Max said. "Korin the weird bird robot. Go back upstairs to the bridge. We need you to navigate not loiter."

From his shoulder Scruff hissed at the robotic creature, putting an exclamation point on Max's order.

"Tiim ezen," the automaton said. Then it turned around and left the room it was in and headed back along the hall.

Max followed.

When they arrived at the bridge Trina looked up from her chair. She was leaning back with big circles under her eyes, looking exhausted. "Where was it?" she asked.

"Down in the lower deck, walking from room to room."

"What was it doing?"

"I'm not sure," he replied. He looked to the metal bird creature. "What were you doing?" he asked it.

It just stood there, staring into space with black glassy eyes.

"Korin, what were you doing walking around in the ship?" he asked.

"Zuraglal," it replied.

Trina looked to him, her eyes heavily lidded. "Well?"

"He says he was mapping," Max said. "Did you sleep last night? Like at all?"

Trina looked away. "Not really... I was worried."

He nodded. "Ok, well as soon as we get going, you go sleep. I'll watch this little metal interloper. Sound good?"

Trina nodded.

"Alright, Korin. We want to go to the fortress of Gelra on the continent of Larana,"

"Larana ül medegdekh," the bird creature said, flapping its comically weak looking metal wings.

"Do you know directions? The big continent to the west of here... Uh... Baruun talaar gazar." Max said.

Korin put a hand to the top of its metal head. "Baruun Gazar. Dalai deegüür üü?"

Trina looked to Max, "What is it saying?"

"It's asking if it's over the ocean. Yes! Yes it's over the ocean," Max said. "That's how you get to another continent."

"Uhm... I can just start going west if you want!" Tela offered. "We need to get out of these mountains first."

"Sure Tela, do that," Max said. He couldn't help but feel like the automaton was dicking with him. Nothing was this stupid, even demonic robot. Especially a demonic robot.

"Dalan garchig telligs," the robot said, nodding its head.

"Seventy telligs?" Max asked.

"That's a heading!" Tela said. "The word we use is Tenik but I know it's the same. Shall we go?"

"Yes Tela," Trina said, yawning with the back of her wrist over her mouth. "I'm going to go... try to sleep."

"Yes!" Max said. "Please do."

Trina left and Max took her seat in one of the two raised chairs with the best view of the front of the ship but he kept an eye on the robot. "Korin, how long?"

"Urt bish," the robot replied. It turned and started walking out the door.

"What do you mean 'not long'? That's not very useful," Max said. "Hey, wait up."

The robot stopped in the doorway, its odd birdlike head turned to look at Max.

"Korin, How long to cross the Hylan ocean, at the cruise speed of this ship?" he asked.

"Kher khurdan," the robot asked. How fast.

"Tela, what is this ship's cruise speed?"

"Seventy seven eken," Tela said.

The automaton looked to the console and then back at Max. "Dörvön ödör," it said.

"Four days!?!" Max asked. "I hope Trina brought food."

Max looked down at his wrist, bringing up his countdown. Ok... he had under nineteen days now, but he'd be fine if this took four days. There would still be more than a week to find Arinna and get her to do whatever it took to make the countdown go away. Man, he might even get to go home. Did he want that?

Maybe. Maybe she'd want come too. No. That was stupid.

Korin took another clanking step out of the bridge.

"Where do you think you're going?" Max asked it. "Stay here where I can see you," Max said. "Go sit over there." He pointed at the wall.

Korin looked at him, then at the wall. There was a pause like it was deciding whether it was worth it to obey, then it went to where Max had indicated.

Max didn't like it. The thing was acting weird. But maybe he would too after a thousand years of rust. Brittney was that old and she had a few screws loose, that's for damned sure, though Max had an inkling she might have always been that way.

"How's it going Tela?" Max asked.

"It's great!" she replied. "I've brought us out of the mountains and matched the heading your little metal friend gave. The weather is clear and the stars are out. It's beautiful."

"It is," Max said, nodding. Though his eyes saw fewer colors at night than he remembered as a human, he saw very well and what he saw was pretty amazing. Clouds of stars filled the sky, innumerable numbers of them. There were a few clouds to the right, hanging over the city they'd raided earlier and Max could see searchlights also, scouring the ground and the skies for the thieving pirates that he'd aided.

Max looked back to the weird automaton which had slid down along the wall and wrapped stick-like metal arms around its knees. It was staring at him with those beady black eyes. He couldn't help but feel a sense of profound unease.

Max sighed, trying to release some of the tension from the day's insanity. He looked out at the stars again.

"Arinna, hold on. I'm coming."

"I'M REALLY surprised you two made friends so quickly. I thought for sure I wouldn't make it in time and the barbarian would be dead," the woman said. She was wearing a mage's robes with a hood draped over the top third of her face and she was talking like she was familiar with him.

What he could see, Raeg didn't recognize. Not that there was anyone he would remember. So far, aside from scattered fragments here and there, and a vague sense of missing something, he hadn't seen anyone he knew.

The dragon woman stroked his head again. "He is strong... and he held me," she said. "I haven't been held in so long."

Raeg shrugged. "What can I say. Chicks dig tattoos."

The woman in the hood, almost cracked a smile at that one. She approached him.

"Ho ho... No," Raeg said. "Your voice sounds familiar, I think, but I don't remember anyone. So keep your distance."

"She is not your enemy, unless you make her one," the dragon woman said, her body pressed against his. Raeg had never had much of a thing for dragons but she was growing on him. It was too bad he was dead. Nothing like that worked, he'd already asked, twice.

The woman pulled back her hood. "If you let me approach you. I can fix that," she said. "I can help you remember."

"Maybe I don't wanna remember," Raeg said. "I was in the line for regret." He put a fist on his chest. "I can feel that, right here. They tell me there's no heart in there but I still feel it."

"I know," she said, taking a step forward. "I was in that line too. I left friends behind... and... maybe I died too easily. Maybe I should have tried harder. I let people down. One of those people was you Raeg, and Max."

"You know me?" he asked. "Uh.. knew me?"

"I did," she said, taking an amulet shaped like a glowing skull from a pouch at her waist. "This will help you remember."

"I don't want the hurt," he said.

"We don't get to choose," she replied.

"She helped me remember," the dragon woman said. "My name is Uul. I come from a land called Saaral. I was hatched there and lived happily, feeding on the mountain sheep and the fish in the clear rivers. It was hard to find a mate. We dragons were few then, and the dragon slayers many. They tracked me down and killed me in my lair while I slept before I'd even had a single hatchling of my own," she said, stroking Raeg's shoulder. "Our pain is part of what makes us who we are, embrace it."

Raeg looked back at the other woman. "Alright," he said. "Let's do it."

The woman approached and held the skull aloft, facing Raeg. Its eyes looked into his and as she held it up, they began to glow.

"Gazric, god of power, want, knowledge, and decay... bringer of the night, bringer of death and doom," she said. As she did, the eyes of the skull changed to purple, then blue-green, then silver, and finally to a deep verdant green.

A skull with green eyes. It held some meaning to him... but Raeg couldn't remember.

"Grant him the sight into his previous incarnation. Let him know who he has become," she said.

"Kharankhuin zakhiragch minii khüsliig biyelüül!" She said.

Then with a hot light, the skull changed again... the colors flickered and merged into an odd glowing black that pulsed once before flooding into him like hot soup poured into a waiting, empty cup.

His life in the north. His mother, and his kin. He was scorned, hated, bullied. He bullied them back. He made them pay. He didn't care what anyone thought. Axes, chopping wood, working it, learning, growing. He became a man, but he was still hated, still despised. In his pain and frustration he sought the dark and it came. Power. Barbaric power. He took much, too much. Too much drink, wealth, and women. It came and went, many times. But there was one he truly loved. He lost her when he was far away. She was in the wrong place at the wrong time, an innocent victim of a brawl over potions.

He mourned her and found out soon after she'd had a son. His son, left with his grandmother to be raised. Raeg was too young, too selfish and ravenous for power. He'd made many mistakes, lost and won many battles but his only true regret was the boy. He should have raised him.

He never saw the man his son became.

Then caught, accused, imprisoned. The mines. Rocks cracking and cracking until a man might go mad from it. Many did, he saw. Many took their own lives. With some help from a friendly stranger he found a way out and ran. Rumors about a necromancer. He found him, hiding in a cave. He killed him and his skeleton minions and took his things. Little was there except for him: Max. The one who who named himself The Boneknight. A good man. A little weird, but a friend.

Raeg stared ahead, feeling again the arms around him.

"You were shaking," Uul said.

Raeg looked at the other woman. "Cheren."

She nodded. "Yes."

"My mother... my... wife," Raeg said. "Are they here?"

Cheren nodded. "Yes, chances are good."

Raeg stood. "I have to go to them... I have to..."

"They're in the lines Raeg," Uul said. "Like all souls. The underworld is broken, destroyed by the very demons charged with protecting it. Souls are eaten or chosen at random for reincarnation. There is no reason here, no system to guide souls through to their proper path."

"She's right," Cheren said. "But you can help us help them. This place can be fixed."

"How?" Raeg said. "The king left! He's never coming back. It's all his fault!"

"No!" said a wavering voice followed by the clack of a cane. It was the old man from before, but now the voice brought back memories from his life. "Gazric was forced to leave this place as part of a deal, an unholy pact with something terrible, something from another plane."

"You're that lich right?" Raeg said. "Melbax?"

"Melnax," Cheren corrected, sighing.

"You look like you've seen better days," Raeg said.

"That is the price of defying death through magic," Melnax said, as he approached, his cane clacking against the broken stone. "My soul is now frail and feeble, but my mind remains."

"He found me and brought my memories back," Cheren said. "There are others here, others loyal to Gazric who want to return this place to what it once was, what it's meant to be: a place where living experiences are processed and souls are prepared for their journey, wherever that may be."

"Divajin," Raeg said.

"Gone," Melnax whispered. "Closed off to all until the passage is restored. Assuming it's even still there."

Raeg looked at his hands. "I... think I might have been killing people like you."

"Death for the dead is not what you think. The demons in control here grow fat on the power of the souls they burn in their furnaces but the essence isn't destroyed, not completely."

"Uh... I feel a little better," Raeg said. "Maybe."

"This can all be fixed," Cheren said. "We need to free Arinna. She has to get here and assume the mantle of her father."

"She is the only one," Melnax said. "But she cannot free herself. A champion must do so, a warrior of the dark."

"Max," Raeg said.

"Yes," Cheren replied. "You... wouldn't know if he has Mytten, would you?" she asked.

"No," Raeg replied, then the memory of what she was talking about caused an involuntary shiver to flutter through his spine. "That's the big spider right?"

"Yes."

"I don't know. He took your things... but we never got to really go through them. I don't know."

Uul patted his shoulder. "It's alright," she said.

"There is something you can do here Raeg. Something important," Melnax said. "I've wanted to try but..."

"Melnax is spent and I'm not strong enough," Cheren said. "My magic alone isn't enough."

"What is it?" Raeg said.

"The avatar of the king has been thrown in a cell in the administrative center," Uul said, her lip curled in a savage snarl.

"Who's that?" Raeg asked.

"He is an important demon tasked with aiding chosen dark warriors," Melnax said, resting himself against a pile of rubble. "He was imprisoned a short time ago. I believe many demons are in league with the light. Without the aid of the king's avatar, the Boneknight will surely fail."

"So... this is a prison break?" Raeg asked.

Cheren nodded.

Raeg grinned. "I'm in... What's this guy's name?"

"He is Vishellus Carcharus Eyran," Cheren said, "but most people know him as The Scragger."

Raeg's face fell. "I'm out."

20

A NAP AND SOME CRAB SALAD

With the robot completely immobile for a number of hours, Max slipped away to check up on Trina and Mytten. Both were sleeping like logs, which was good.

Just looking at poor Mytten with those missing limbs made him feel sad and angry, though not so much at the knights who'd done it as himself. This was his fault. He'd left to steal that ship for the pirates and now, for the second time, Mytten was a casualty.

He wanted this to be over. They had to get to Arinna. They had to find her and free her... and... hopefully she'd know what to do then, because he sure didn't.

On the other hand, Max wasn't sure he even wanted to go home at this point, even if what that weird cat/dog angel thing had said was true. He wanted to see this through and if he was being honest with himself, he wanted to see her again. Arinna was beautiful in that dangerous scary kind of way. Sure, she was only about ten thousand years older than he was, but hey... did that really matter when you're both dead?

He had no idea how old she really was, or who her mother was. She could be three thousand years old or three hundred thousand. Who knew. At this point, anything was possible.

One thing was for sure: he wasn't going to ask a god how old she was, at least not directly. Maybe Vish would know, if Max ever saw him again.

He went back up to the bridge, checking on the creepy metal parrot. It was still there, in exactly the same position as before. The airship was still cruising over open ocean with nothing to be seen from the bridge view port but stars and the black water beneath. There should still be a few hours until daybreak, maybe he could study up on his stuff a little.

He glanced at the demon parrot again. Still immobile. Alright, everything seemed good.

Max sat back down in the chair and brought up his status display. He'd gotten a few cool things. There was that loot box, a new spell, though it didn't show up on his status screen, and of course... that wicked looking giant sword.

First things first. He hovered over the spells list. There was an ellipsis at the end of it, meaning there were more in there, but he couldn't see them. When he pressed the ellipsis nothing happened, but then he tried the word "Magic" and a whole new screen came up.

```
Magic

• Ball of Flame • Bolt Lance • Dead Weight
• Flame • Freeze • Ground Slam
• One with the Void • Shock • Sleep
• Stagnation • Teeth of Fate • Void Crush
```

"Hell... how did I miss this?" he asked himself. Then he thought about it, the book had mentioned the magic screen. He'd just thought it was talking about the main status. Duh.

It listed all his spells and let him hover over them to see a window with their effects. Very nice. Very useful, especially for the future. If he ended up staying in this place after they got to Arinna, he could see himself using a lot more magic. That had always been one of his favorite parts of games in the past and now that he was starting to get a good list of different spells it was becoming exponentially more interesting.

"Let's see... what's the new one. Oh," he said. There were actually two. Both looked to have been generated by his betrothed label as they were time and space related, that seemed to be the theme with those. The first was called Stagnation. He hovered over it.

Stagnation: When cast upon one enemy target this spell lowers the targets agility and strength scores by

the caster's mind score added to caster skill level divided by two. Duration in seconds is determined by caster skill level divided by ten with a minimum of ten but is halved if target resists dark magic. Cost: 101 mp.

"Ooh, pricey, but nice," he said. Not only did it slow the target and make them easier to hit, because agility effected both evasion and combat speed, but it lowered their strength just as much, making their attacks weaker. This was a neutering spell, plain and simple. The best part was that even if something resisted it, the effect halved in duration, not power. Sweet. That made it significantly better than sleep, which if the enemy resisted it, just didn't work.

He then hovered over the second spell.

One with the Void: The caster is teleported into a pocket dimension where the caster is invisible, cannot see enemies and cannot make attacks or be attacked. While in this dimension mana is drained from enemies to the caster in the area of effect. This drain effect only happens once regardless of the length of time in the void. Area of mana drain effect is 126 filgreths plus 2 filgreths per skill level of caster. Cost: 77 mp plus any additional used. Duration: caster may remain in the void for a number of seconds equal to caster skill level divided by three. Limited use: once per night.

"Nice, nice," he said. So this was a way to get back MP and avoid being damaged at the same time. He needed that. The area of effect seemed to be a little over ten feet and that expanded with his class skill, which was good. Getting back magic points was difficult in this world. It required either black potions which were expensive and difficult to obtain, sleeping which made you an insta-kill basically, or a maybe having an entire battle from inside a pile of noxious rotting entrails. That last one might be worth trying sometime if he could keep the crawlers from eating it.

That reminded him, he looked over at his dungeon crawler. The creature had been pretty quiet since he returned to the ship. Then he heard a tiny snore. Like Trina and Mytten, Scruff was passed out.

Max patted the little tentacle monster on the head. "Adorable," he said.

He looked back at the demonic automaton, in the corner. Still nothing.

He still had the books for Venom, Empower, and Hasten to use but he would want to be Dark Mage for that. There was also the sword.

Yeah... he had to check out the sword.

He opened up his equipment screen and tried to equip it.

Bzzzt!

"What?" Max snapped. "But... but this is..." Oh wait. He'd switched to Breeder to talk to Scruff. Breeder was a vitality class in the Decay affinity, two handed weapons were limited to the ambition ones. He'd probably have to switch back to Mercenary to try it out. He'd only switched like an hour ago, it might give him problems. Was it worth it for a big ultra violent two-handed sword called The Flesh Ripper?

Yes. Yes it was.

He brought up his equipment screen and yanked all his leather armor, then switched to the class selection screen and pressed Mercenary.

The switch over was painless. No headache, no queasy stomach, he was good.

Back to the equipment and...

Bzzzt!

"Shit!" Max said. "What the hell? Is this thing class limited or something? Oh."

It was obvious. Games tended to give you items that connected to one another. He wasn't sure how that was possible in a real world with game-like mechanics, but there it was. He was willing to bet the class that resulted from that skull in his inventory would be able to use the sword.

Dread Knight. Had to be.

People had been wondering if he was a Dread Knight for a while now, ever since the first time he went into that human village and met Wyk. It might be the perfect class for an undead, something with abilities that meshed well with his immunities and weaknesses. Or it could just look cool as hell, which would also be Ok.

"Well... I guess I can't do that," he said.

There was no chance he'd try out a class upgrade again, not right away. Arinna was right there. He was actually starting to feel the pull toward her again, at least he thought he was. If he screwed up a class upgrade there was no telling what might happen. It was too much of a risk.

"Back to Dark Mage," he said, brought up the screen and switched.

He almost fell over. The vertigo hit him like a rock to the skull. Everything was spinning like the day after the worst bender ever. He held on to his chair. Would he even be able to walk?

He just sat, leaning back in his chair, waiting for it to go away but he couldn't think about anything but how horrible he felt. It had to be the big swing in mind points... or maybe just too many changes too fast... Gah. This was bad.

He had to do something.

The sleep symbol... he could crawl there... Or maybe he could cast sleep on himself.

0/366 MP

"Dammit," he cursed. Why zero?

He flopped onto the floor and crawled on his skeletal hands and boney knees, out of the bridge and down the hall. He didn't want to annoy Trina or Mytten with this. He'd worry them for no reason and they needed to sleep. He just needed an analgesic, but in a world where they didn't exist and he didn't have any flesh anyway, the sleep rune would do.

It seemed to take forever as he dragged himself around the corner, past three of the scruffs who were gnawing on bones in a different cabin, before he arrived at the room with the rune on the floor.

Scruff hissed.

Max looked over at him. "Oh... sorry buddy. I guess I woke you," he said. But the crawler was facing behind him.

It took everything he had, while his head pounded and his vision whirled in circles, to turn around enough to see what was there.

It was the automaton.

Before Max could say anything, there was a ting of spring-loaded action as the rusted metal creature vaulted forward and pushed him and scruff backward into the rune.

Everything went dark.

~

SOMETHING in the distance was knocking, loudly. Wait no, it wasn't far away, it was close, really close. It was his skull!

Trina was hanging over him, banging her fist on Max's forehead.

"Wake up bonehead!" she said. "Something's happened!"

Yes, Trina was right. Something had happened! He'd changed classes and ended up with a bad switch. Then he tried to crawl to the sleep rune and...

That damned robot!

"The robot!" Max yelled, sitting up too fast and knocking his skull into Trina's forehead.

"Ow!" she said. "You idiot!"

"Sorry... I..." he looked down, he was wearing the Dark Mage robe and boots.

"I took the liberty of equipping it for you," she said. " It was a pain too. I had to try all your clothes one at a time because you look the same no matter what class you are... and... you were lying here... you know."

"I get it," he said. She could do that? He supposed he could do it to her, so it only made sense it went both ways. "Where is the robot?" he asked.

"I don't know but-"

CLANG.

The whole ship shook.

“What was that?!” Max asked.

“I don't know! It's why I woke you up!,” Trina replied. “We're on the ground.”

“We're what? Why?” he asked.

“If I knew that, I would have told you!” Trina snapped back. “Come on.”

“Wait!” Max said, grabbing her shoulder as he checked his magic.

366/366 MP

“What?” she asked.

“You check the bridge. Ask Tela what happened and find the robot... er... the automaton if you can,” Max said.

CLANG. CLANG!

“And you're going outside?” she asked.

Max nodded. “Wish me luck.”

“Good luck. Don't die,” she said.

She went right and Max went left.

“Do my best,” he mumbled under his breath as he jogged to the back where the cargo bay ramp was. Scruff was in the bay waving his tentacles like a madman.

“Look I can't hear you now buddy,” Max said. “I switched again.”

Scruff's tentacles went limp.

"Sorry," Max replied as he entered the bay and pulled the lever that released the door. "Look, stay here. I'm going to have a look outside... holy crabs!"

There were crabs outside the ship, by the hundreds... no thousands. They were part pink and part blue with giant pincer claws. The only difference from the ones back on Earth was that these were a little weird. The eye stalks came out of a bump a little ways back on the shell instead of the front and it seemed like they might have fewer legs than the kind he was used to. Otherwise, you'd never know the difference. They were spiky, clawed, and angry.

As soon as Max hit the release to open the bay door, they started to flood in from the outside washing up from the sandy beach beyond like spiky waves.

"Crap, crap, crap!" he yelled. He didn't want them inside doing who knows what to the ship. "Scruff, close the door!"

Scruff made a salute-like gesture and began crawling up the wall toward the crank lever. Max didn't know how the dungeon crawler was going to crank a lever with a bunch of tentacles, but he wasn't about to ask either. Scruff seemed confident, that was enough.

That left only one thing for Max to do.

"Time to make a crab salad!"

What spell to use? The crabs were all wet after having come out of the ocean. Lightning wouldn't be a bad choice but

Bolt lance, despite having excellent damage potential, was really a cutting kind of spell. It had a heavy discharge that went fast and didn't spread.

No, it was Shock time. Shock was level one like Flame. It had a lower raw damage potential than the fire spell but rather than pumping up with more magic points it fired continuously if you kept using it.

“This ought to do extra damage to you guys,” Max said to the crabs. They didn't respond at all. They just kept climbing into the ship.

Max extended his hands and aqua blue lightning arced out but instead of to the crabs, it curved and went right into the ship's metal ramp, burning a black line along the floor and filling the cargo bay with the smell of ozone. Duh, most of the ship was made of metal, lightning inside was not a good idea.

“I should have seen that coming,” he said, sighing. “New plan.”

Max started punting the crabs out of the door. His strength wasn't super high as a mage to begin with but the bonus from his signet ring helped a lot. These crabs were only about the size of small dogs so it wasn't too hard to make some headway, especially when the ramp started raising. He punted the last four crabs out when the ramp was about seventy-five percent raised.

“Thanks Scruff,” he called back. “I'm gonna regret this,” he added and dove out through the opening.

Outside was the worst nightmare of a person with a seafood allergy. The Midnight was parked on the beach of an insanely tiny island, like a sand bar really. The island was crescent shaped with no vegetation whatsoever. The only thing on the island were crabs, monstrous crabs, everywhere, all streaming toward their ship.

Three of them tried to clamp onto Max's legs but he kicked them away.

"Plan C, I guess," he said.

Flame time.

Max pumped the fire up to basketball size and tossed it into the middle of the crabs. The fireball exploded, flash cooking the crabs in a five foot radius but it was nothing, not even a dent in their numbers.

CLANG!

That noise again. It was coming from the front of the ship. Max threw a second and then a third flame ball, clearing himself a path.

"Man it's too bad I'm not human right now because I bet these guys taste amazing," he said as he made it around the right propeller spar and... holy...

Max's jaw dropped.

A twenty foot wide crab was butted up to the front of the airship. Max watched as it raised a huge eight foot long claw and smashed it on the front of the ship.

CLANG!

“Hey!” Max yelled at it. “I had to do a lot of crazy shit to get that ship. Get the hell away!”

Bolt lance.

The blast of lightning fired out in a perfect line. The magic neatly severed the crab's left claw which dropped to the sand with a loud thump. Immediately the monstrous creature turned to face Max, rising up and waving its other claw in a threat display.

“Oh yeah?” Max said. “Think you're big and tough? Try this on for size,” he said.

Void Crush.

Max pumped an extra seventy points of magic into the black orb between his hands while imagining the center of the crabs shell. The orb short forward, disappearing inside the creature. Then about two seconds later there was huge crack as a perfect sphere of the crab crunched in its center, ripping free and causing a flood of noxious looking green and blue liquid to dribble out of the bottom of the car sized crab shell. The creature dropped to the sand, dead.

No sooner had Max dispatched the big one, than two more were latching on to his heels.

14 damage received.

7 damage received.

Now that he was outside Shock was the perfect solution.

The aqua blue electricity fried both crabs in seconds as well as the fourteen or so others in Max's general vicinity as he waved the lightning around zapping every crab in range.

They kept coming though, worse, they seemed to be enjoying the bodies he'd created. Scores of crabs were fighting to get to the other dead crabs. They were ripping into them with their claws and stuffing chunks of their dead fellows into their jointed, insect-like, mouth parts as fast as possible.

"Max!" Trina called. Her head and shoulders were sticking out of the hatch on the top of the ship.

Max waved. "It's crabs!" he yelled.

"I see that!" she called back. "Tela's not responding. I can't get her to come back. The whole ship is dead."

"Awesome," Max said, zapping another group of crabs until they sizzled. "Where's the damned automaton?"

"I don't know. I searched the ship and..." she paused, pointing emphatically to Max's right. "There! I see him!"

Max looked out where Trina was pointing. There, on the far end of the sandbar, way, way out, was the bird-like robot.

"When the hell did he go out there?" Max said. "Dammit!" He looked back to Trina. "I see him, I'm going after him."

"Go fast!" she yelled as she threw two bombs off the side of the ship. They detonated and took scores of crabs with them but it wasn't even close to affecting their numbers.

"They're piling up higher, soon they'll be prying the view ports off!"

"Gotcha," Max said, running forward with Shock blasting away, frying every crab it came in contact with. Though, something he saw near the ship had him veer to the side for a second. One of Trina's explosions had blasted big enough to break apart some of the giant crab's remains and something was shining near the bottom of it.

It was an item drop, had to be.

"It may be the stupidest thing I do all day," he mumbled to himself. "But I'm not gonna leave behind a rare drop."

He used Shock to clear a path but the crabs were thickest near the giant dead one. They were all fighting to consume its remains. So Max lobbed a fireball right into the middle of them. The resulting explosion was large enough to shake the ship, prompting Trina to yell some thing at him, but he couldn't pay attention. He was too intent on threading his way through the crab guts to get to where he thought he saw the.... There it was! It was a book!

21

DEMONIC TORTURE AND A KAIJU BATTLE

Raeg and his fellow conspirators hid behind what looked like an overturned food stall, long ago emptied and smashed. Ahead of them, barricades had been erected but were mostly derelict. Only a few heads and glowing eyes could be seen walking the battlements. The building, though battered and crumbling, looked more heavily guarded and secured than any mansion or lords manor Raeg had seen.

"This looks like a prison," Raeg said.

"For workers, yes," Melnax replied. "Vishellus is only there to keep him close to the cabal of demons who are currently running this place. They'll be draining his power until he's weak, then they'll devour him."

Raeg grumbled. "Maybe that's for the best."

"Raeg!" Cheren said.

"I don't trust that flying eye," Raeg said.

"You don't have to," Cheren said. "Trust me. I died with you and your friend, remember?"

Raeg grumbled again. "Yes," he replied as if spitting the words. "So how long are we going to wait here?"

"I thought you didn't want to go!" Cheren retorted.

"I hate waiting," he said.

"Ah... here they are," Melnax said.

"Where?" Raeg asked, turning a circle. "I don't see anyone."

Then a roar sounded from Raeg's right as a line of souls, creatures of the dark all, rose and called a challenge to the walls of the ruined fortress before them. Glowing eyes of every one of the four affinities of the dark pierced the gloom, creating a line of menace, headed by Uul the dragon woman.

Raeg saw her and waved and she waved in return.

"Don't wave you fool!" Cheren said. "You'll give us away. We're supposed to go in the side entrance."

Raeg shrugged. "I like her," he said. Then he turned to the old hooded man. "Where they keepin' him?"

"I'm coming with you. I must-"

"No," Raeg said, putting a hand on Melnax's shoulder. "You've done enough and we'll need to move fast. Just tell us."

“He will be four floors down,” Melnax replied. “That is what I was told. But you must beware... the demons in that building are incredibly strong. They've been feeding on souls for centuries.”

The roar reached a fever pitch, but it was answered only by the sound of boots and clawed feet pounding against stone as the building guards rushed to man the piecemeal walls they defended.

“URAGSHAA!” Uul shouted and the small army of snarling dark creatures of every description flew, ran, loped, and slithered toward the walls.

Balls of black fire rained down from above, immolating those unfortunate enough be caught their way, but the charge continued.

Raeg wanted to go with them. He yearned for his axes, for the thrill of chopping the enemy apart but Cheren gripped his arm.

“No,” she said. “This way.”

She led him down into a tunnel that went under the street and emerged on the other side. Two guards stood ahead of them. They weren't demons but regular souls pressed into service. Each held something that looked like a crooked spear.

“Hold up your tag,” Cheren said, holding up one of her own.

“Huh? Oh.” Raeg said.

"You're coming in to work late!" one of the guards said.

"Yeah, you know how it is," Raeg replied. "Demons ask for the stupidest shit."

The guard on the left nodded. "Don't I know it."

"There a riot goin on?" the first guard asked. He looked like he might have been an orc once, long ago, but now had been twisted into grisly form.

"Yeah," Raeg replied. "I'd kinda like to get in before they get over here."

"Ohhhhh. That's too bad. We can't let anyone in when there's a riot," said the second one. "That's an absolute no, no."

The first guard nodded. "Absolutely."

Raeg shook his head and smashed a fist into each of their faces at the same time. They dropped like bags of rotten fish heads on a wet dock. He looked at the black spear-like weapons.

"Is it worth it taking one of those?"

"No," Cheren said as she took the keys to the gate ahead from the neck of a downed guard. "They give them out to make them feel important."

Raeg nodded. "Ah." He scratched his head. "But... if it's so easy to get inside here, why didn't you break in before?"

"The demons," Cheren said as she unlatched the gate and slipped inside. "You'll see."

Entering the complex was actually pretty easy. It was almost deserted inside. There were a few demons and bound and unbound souls walking about, but they paid them no mind. As a Barbarian and a Dark Mage, Raeg and Cheren didn't look that different from the rest of them and that probably helped.

Everything went fine until they found the stairs and began descending to the lower floor. They hadn't walked more than ten steps when Raeg heard the door close behind them.

"Raeg!" said a familiar smarmy voice. Vigolos.

"What?" Raeg said, sounding annoyed. It was the truth too, this whole place annoyed the hell out of him.

The Dark elf was standing above him on the stairs. "Who sent you down here? You were supposed to come to me if you survive... eh... defeated the woman." He frowned. "Who is this?"

Cheren turned, raising her hands to prepare some kind of spell but Raeg grabbed her wrist, stopping her. Then he let her go and took a step up the stairs.

"Uul," Raeg said. "Her name was Uul."

"I know her name," Vigolos said, frowning. "You have to report to me when you finish a job. I need to know what my inferiors are up to so I can file the proper paperwork, otherwise the weekly audits become a literal waking nightmare."

Raeg shook his head. "I don't know what you're talking about, but I don't care." Then he lunged and slammed a fist in Vigolos's stomach causing the elf to wheeze like an old man. Raeg grabbed the elf's head with both hands and brought it down into his knee with a crack. The elf went limp, knocked out cold. Raeg then ripped the tag off and dropped the pointy-eared administrator to the floor. The dark elf's limp form then slid head first down half the flight of stairs, dragging his arms behind him.

Cheren was standing there, her mouth hanging open. "You are a violent man."

"Yep," Raeg replied. "Let's go."

Down they went, three more levels to sub-level four. They encountered no one else on the way, not until they arrived on the bottom floor.

A Demon stood guard at the door. He was easily two feet taller than Raeg with curled horns, a long spiked tail, and even wings on his back. He looked bored.

"State your business," he barked as they approached.

"Uh..." Cheren said.

Raeg looked at her. She was pretty enough. It might work.

"Last request for Vishellus," Raeg said.

The demon frowned. "Most irregular... and as you know there's no point. We are not of the flesh and cannot-"

"I know!" Raeg growled. "Don't you think I damned well know?"

"Then why are you bringing him a woman?" the demon demanded.

"By Barghel's beard, he's The Scragger! I was told he just likes to talk to them, you know... be friends."

The disgusted look on the demon's face said everything. He had no words and waved them on.

When they were inside Cheren pulled on his arm. "What's so gross about being friends?" she asked.

"If you have to ask," Raeg replied. "You wouldn't get it if I told ya."

She frowned.

From the distance, they heard a high-pitched scream.

"No! They're torturing a child!" Cheren said.

Raeg shook his head as they jogged down the hall to a partially open door. "I don't think so," he said.

Another blood curdling scream rang out from inside the room as Cheren and Raeg peeked inside.

Of course, as Raeg had expected, the screams were coming from the Scragger. He was strung out at an angle, tied by his hands and feet to bright metal braces with a shiny light metal collar around his neck.

"How did they get Sun steel down here?" Cheren whispered.

There was a huge demon standing over the Scragger. The beast's toothy maw curled into a gleeful grin as it used a tiny feather to tickle the eye demon's armpit.

"Eeeeeeeeek!" Vishellus cried as a stream of black liquid poured out of his lower region. "Please... please no more."

"Oh? Oh? No more what? You mean this?" the great demon said and tickled him again.

The Scragger struggled to free himself, but soon was forced into another shriek, followed by another emission of the same black fluid which dribbled into a catch pan beneath him.

Raeg couldn't believe what he was seeing. He was going to throw up.

Cheren pulled him away from the door, whispering. "That demon is huge and powerful. We need a plan to get him out."

Raeg grimaced. There was no way he was going sit here, talking, while that was going on in there. Just hearing it again was too much. It had to be stopped, for his own sanity.

"I got yer plan," he said and barged through the door.

"Hey!" the demon cried, its smile fading. "Who are you? How dare you interrupt my fun!"

Raeg walked right up to the demon and smashed a fist into its face. The creature was too stunned to do anything but cover its aching face.

That helped a lot. In Raeg's opinion, the best thing an opponent could do in response to an attack was hide their face. It made it incredibly easy to punch them everywhere else, which he did. He kept bashing and pummeling and smashing until the creature finally fell to the floor, begging him to stop.

When Raeg turned around, Cheren had already freed the small winged demon. Throwing the Sun steel collar to the floor.

The Scragger was staring at Raeg. "In all my dreams of escape. Never once did I imagine it would be you," he said.

"Yeah, well I'm no fan of this either." Raeg pointed a finger at Cheren. "She talked me into it."

"Thank you both," the creature said, rubbing his wrists. Then he leaned down toward the container of black liquid.

Raeg frowned. "Get away from that! What are you doing with it?!"

"It's my soul energy," Vishellus replied. "I'm going to drink it, of course."

Raeg whirled around, covering his mouth. "Ugh.... No! I'm gonna be sick."

The sound of slurping followed, and it lasted far longer than Raeg would have liked.

"Let's get out of here," Cheren said.

"Don't worry, now that you've removed that collar, I can teleport at any time," Vishellus said. "I need to get to Max immediately. One of my former colleagues came and bragged that he's been manipulating an automaton in a plan to kill him. But first, we need to go upstairs to my office. There's something I must retrieve. Take hold of my hands."

Raeg shook his head. "No."

"Do it!" Cheren growled through her teeth.

How could she ask this? Didn't she hear what that disgusting thing just did?

Raeg grimaced and slid forward, stretching out a finger to touch the demon's grubby, clawed, little mitt.

There was a poof of smoke and they were gone.

MAX BENT DOWN and snatched the tome from the sand.

Acquired: Thundercrack.

The book had a shiny lightning bolt on the cover and some writing, but there wasn't time to read it, so he stored it and continued on, switching back to Shock to cut a swath through the crabs in order to get out to the end of the sandbar where the robot was currently hanging out.

There were fewer crabs out here. It seemed relatively quiet in comparison. The only thing around was the robot and the only sound was the waves, softly washing against the beach.

"Korin, you little ass, Get back to the ship and turn it on!" Max snapped. "Before I fry you like a corn-dog."

The bird head turned and began laughing. The sound was chilling.

"You fool," said a voice. This was the first time Max had heard the robot speak anything other than High Demonic, and the voice was different too, no more tinny metallic noise, just a smooth, deep voice. "Did you think we'd allow a human to free her?"

"Oh..." Max said. Now everything made sense.

The robot leaned back and screeched.

Max couldn't believe the power of the piercing sound. Even without ears it hurt his head.

"What are you doing?!" he yelled.

The automaton turned to face Max. "I have summoned the guardian of this dungeon."

Max looked around. A dungeon? Where? Wait... no, that wasn't too surprising. First Fantasy loved to hide dungeons in hard to get places. Usually you needed to be there at a certain time of day or have a special item or something and only then it would open. Or... sometimes... you had to fight a monster.

"I chose this place specifically for you, Max. It's a water creature of the light, purity through and through. It will devour your worthless decaying bones and dissolve you into oblivion."

"What's your name?" Max asked.

The automaton laughed. "I'll enjoy watching you die."

There was a rumble beneath Max's feet. The sand seemed to be vibrating, the water too. There were circles rolling along the waves, centered about two hundred feet off shore to Max's left. Whatever was coming, it was gigantic.

"Oh... no, no, no," Max said, shaking his head. "I thought this was gonna be a good day!"

He grabbed at the robot but it dodged him, running out into the ocean up to its knees.

"Come any closer and I'll have it dive into the sea, destroying it," the voice said.

The vibration was getting louder. Max could hear a low rumbling noise as well, like whale song, only a thousand times more powerful. It was like a humpback with a garbage truck sized sub-woofer.

Then, to Max's surprise, there was a poof of smoke behind the automaton as Vish appeared from thin air.

"Augh!" Max cried.

Vish waved and used his claws to quickly open a panel on the back of the robot, ripping something small and wriggling out, which he threw into the sea.

The bird automaton instantly looked around. It seemed to note with some distress that it was up to its hips in sea water and immediately began exiting the ocean.

Max ran up to the eye demon. “Vish! What happened to you?!”

“There's no time to explain,” Vish replied. “Quickly, take these. One is for Arinna, it may help her remember herself, and the other is for you.”

The eye demon handed two sealed letters over, which Max took.

Acquired: Letter for Arinna.

Acquired: Letter for Max.

“But... there's so much I need to ask you,” Max said.

“There isn't time,” Vish said. “I'm weak... and there are bad things happening in the underworld. I can't stay here for long. Plus...”

“What?” Max asked. “Plus what?”

“I'm not really supposed to interfere with your journey. I can advise, give a little item here and there, but not affect.”

Max folded his arms. “Seriously? Didn't you kill the paladin Tesh that one time?”

Vish frowned. “I did not! I merely adjusted his fall a tiny bit, mostly for theatrical purposes. Like an art piece. I mean really, wasn't the way his body caught on that church spire just spectacular?”

Max nodded. “It was pretty great... Hey! I met your counterpart the flying puppy thing. She tried to kill me! That seems like interference to me!”

“You saw her?” Vish said, grimacing. “I'm so sorry! Isn't she insufferable?”

“She's fluffy,” Max said.

“Well... yes,” Vish replied.

There was a huge roar as a horrifically large serpentine fish burst from the waves, its rainbow scales caught the light of the morning sun creating a blinding spectacle of light that made Max recoil from its utter brilliance. Water sprayed in all directions as the behemoth's gargantuan body displaced tons and tons of it, causing massive waves to start rolling in toward the shore.

The robot started to run, Max followed it, snatching it up from the beach.

“Yeah I'll be coming back for this dungeon,” he said but when he looked left he saw Vish flapping along side him.

“You said she tried to kill you?” Vish asked.

“Who?” Max asked.

“Vita!” Vish said. “The angel!”

“Oh, right. She was going to, yes... then I scratched her ears and she couldn't.”

“That's good enough,” Vish said as he reached out, touching Max's shoulder.

There was poof of purple smoke as Max and the robot disappeared and arrived inside the ship. Vish was gone but the thumping on the outside of the ship from the piles and piles of crabs was continuing.

"TRINA!" Max yelled.

"Max?" she replied, climbing down from the upper hatch and closing it behind her. "There's a sea monster out there!"

"I know!" he said, then he turned the robot to face him. "Can you fix the ship?"

It nodded.

"Ok, Go!" Max said as he put it down.

"Can we trust it?" Trina asked.

"I dunno... Maybe? Vish tore something out of its head. I think he's better."

"Who?" Trina asked, frowning. "Oh... right. You said you have a demon friend."

The automaton was trundling into the bridge. Max ran along behind it as a deafening roar echoed throughout the ship, shaking the metal like it was a steel drum.

"Just get up front and get ready," Max said.

The metallic bird creature made it to the front console of the ship where it stuck one of its hands under a plate and turned something. Instantly, power returned to the ship.

“-Hey! Don't touch that... Max? Trina?” Tela said, for the first time ever, she sounded a little annoyed. “I think that automaton turned me off!”

“Tela!” Max yelled. “Get us in the air, immediately!”

“Yes, yes, yes!” Trina chimed in.

“Absolutely!” Tela said and the airship hummed to life, rising from the sands.

Max was watching the giant serpent from the front view port and he did not like what he was seeing. It had noticed the ship and was moving in their direction, quickly.

“Faster Tela!” Max said.

“I'm going as quickly as I can!” Tela said happily.

The sea monster was getting close. Its maw could easily bite half the ship off with one chomp.

“I don't think you understand the urgency of the situation!” Max yelled. “Like... If we don't get out of here immediately. WE ARE GOING TO DIE!”

“Ok!” Tela replied. “Wow... You are spirited today, aren't you?”

Max rubbed his skull with his hands.

“Something is holding us down, but I've got it I think,” Tela said cheerfully.

The ship finally tore free of the many many crabs and ascended, turning away from the island. The guardian monster managed to spray a thick stream of water at them, like a water beam, but they just barely made it out of range and the ship was gently showered with spray.

"We're clear!" Tela said.

"Ok, now turn back," Max replied.

"WHAT?" Trina shouted, "You can't be serious!"

Max nodded. "Tela, circle it, just out of range of its water attack."

"Max!" Trina said. "You don't have to do this to impress Arinna."

Max stood up, walking out of the bridge. "No, I don't. I want to do it for myself."

As the ship banked right, Max climbed up to the top hatch, hanging his body out. The monstrous fish creature was still there, bellowing an ear shattering challenge that vibrated the sea around it in perfect concentric rings.

"Max! Come down!" Trina was yelling at him from below. "This is stupid!"

"Just tell Tela to keep doing what I said," he yelled back as he summoned the new spell book into his palm and opened it. The knowledge poured into his eye sockets like bolts of lighting.

He took a long breath. Thundercrack. It was a level three spell, the highest a mage could handle. The magic point cost was staggering, more than ten times what it cost to cast Bolt Lance, but that was just fine. He should have points left, so why not?

Max put his hands together. This would either kick ass or destroy their ship.

“Nothing ventured, nothing gained,” he said as the power charged between his skeletal hands, growing a pulsing ball of hot violet electricity.

The sea serpent was bellowing again. This time it swung its body in an arc, casting some kind of magic that caused pillars of water to erupt from the sea itself. They would have been hit by three of them if Tela hadn't expertly threaded the ship between them.

“MAX!” Trina yelled from below.

He could feel the magic draining as the spell reached full power. “Here we go!” he said and fired.

A wide bolt of electricity exploded from his hands, making an audible boom as it roared across the sky, contacting the great serpentine creature directly in its chin. The spell lasted for five whole seconds as the lightning ran across the creature's jaw and down along the left side of its body, flash-vaporizing everything it touched and leaving a massive winding trail of charred flesh. The monster shook with violent spasms during the discharge and when it ceased the great fish dropped into the sea slack and lifeless.

“Did you get it?” Trina yelled from below.

Hmmm. Maybe. It was level three spell, probably double damage because of the lightning and the fact that the color meant the spell was the power affinity which was good against purity. That would push it up even further, but he wasn't even at Dark Mage level fifty. That mattered, he knew it did. Then there was that other thing...

"I don't think so," he yelled down. "Did you see a notification, because I didn't!"

Then from below he heard Trina yelp and Max looked up to see the charred sea serpent rising from the deep directly ahead of them.

"Uh oh," he said. "Maybe this was a rash decision."

The airship swerved, trying to avoid it but the serpentine creature roared and struck out with a long fin that wrapped around their ship.

Max checked his magic.

1/240 MP

Thundercrack had cost a hundred and twenty. Now he was broke.

"Dammit!" he yelled. "I'm out of juice!"

"Just use a Dark essence!" Trina called from below.

"I would but we don't have those!"

"Yes we do!" Trina yelled back.

Max shrugged and summoned... a small vial filled with black liquid appeared in his hand.

"I'll be damned," he said as he dumped it down his gullet.

Magic restored.

"Alright fish face. Come get some!"

Max summoned the magic, building the crackling sphere of bright violet electricity as the creature lunged forward opening its great maw filled with row upon row of long pointed teeth.

"You've been... Thunderstruck!" Max yelled and with a monstrous crack unleashed the blast at point blank range. The lighting shot into the top of the monster's mouth and bored right through its skull and brain before exploding out the other side.

The fin released its hold on the ship as its lifeless owner slumped into the sea.

You've defeated Gutter Crabs, King Gutter Crab, and Samudra guardian of the Suddara water dungeon.

You've gained a level of Dark Mage!

You've gained a level of Dark Mage!

You've gained a level of Dark Mage!

You've gained a level of Dark Mage!

You've gained a level of Dark Mage!

You've gained a level of Dark Mage!

You've gained a level of Dark Mage!

You've gained a level of Dark Mage!

You've gained a level!

Trina has gained a level of Plague Doctor!

Trina has gained a level!

Suddara water dungeon has been opened.

Max laughed as he climbed down from the top of the ship. "We win! And I got eight more levels of mage! Isn't that awesome?"

"I will never sleep again," Trina said flatly and shook her head as she walked back toward the bridge.

22

A CHANCE ENCOUNTER AND FALLING FOR EACH OTHER

The next three and a half days of flying passed surprisingly quickly. Max used the three other spell books he had, learning all the new spells, but then he switched back to Mercenary. This was Trina's idea as she felt he would have a lower profile and might even be able to walk around Clathia in the Sun Steel armor and gather information unmolested. Max would have preferred to stay a Dark Mage, but Trina had a point. It just sucked that for Mercenary his best weapons were now the old beat up Black iron axe and Brittney's purity dagger which damaged him constantly every time he tried to use it.

Though, the best thing about the journey had been his letter:

Dear Bonehead,

It's Raeg. I'm dead, but I'm not doin' so bad. You should come visit sometime. Ha ha. No don't. Go find that girl first. Give her a hug for me. That flying one-eyed freak told me how important it is that we get someone on the throne here but I've seen it for myself. It's bad here. So get that done. Also, you were right. Bacon is incredible.

Your friend,

Raeg.

P.S. Cheren and Melnax are here too. They say hi.

WHEN MAX READ the last part to Trina, she cried. Max would have cried too, if he could. It was good to know Raeg was okay, and Cheren too. The barbarian's words made Max that much more determined to find Arinna and finish this but it also gave him an idea, something he'd have to think about.

The other letter wouldn't open for him, so that message would have to wait. That was fine, it was for Arinna after all. If things worked out, he could give it to her himself.

As they approached the coast on the morning of the fourth day Max felt strangely at peace. The towers of Gelra loomed in the distance like monstrous swollen teeth, serrated with turrets and bristling with the spears of the warriors stationed there. In the center of them all was the largest, like a fortress of its own. This tower had ringlets and defensive slits going all the way to its jagged peak.

If that wasn't enough, the whole fortress was surrounded by patrolling airships slowly making their way in an endless parade across the sky.

"That must be where they're keeping her," Trina said. "It's logically the strongest point. It's where I would put her."

"I... I don't think so." Max said. The feeling that had guided him before was much weaker now, almost completely gone. He'd felt Arinna's presence for days, which had helped them zero in on the fortress, but it hadn't gotten any stronger. It was like something was blocking it. Maybe they had magic wards here... or... and he hated to think about it: maybe it was whatever they'd put inside her.

Max grit his teeth, feeling the anger well up. Those bastards.

When he'd asked to be dropped in a grassy field near a village and what looked to be a monastery, Trina didn't agree with him, but she'd let him go anyway. As he was about to climb down the ladder she'd handed him a mirror taken from the airship's tiny lavatory.

"Just don't get discovered and when you want to be picked up, flash us with the mirror. We'll be directly to the east over the ocean," she'd said.

"They won't notice an airship just loitering over there?" he'd asked but Trina had assured him they wouldn't be alone. Many foreign merchant ships were hanging in the sky to the east of the coastal city that supported the fortress, waiting for permission to land.

So Max let go of the rope ladder and walked north, toward the towering walled structure that reminded him of a monastery or convent. Something about it felt right. If he were trying to hide someone like Arinna, he wouldn't do it in the obvious place. That place would be a trap. No, it would be somewhere else, somewhere defensible and nearby, but also unassuming. This place fit the bill, perfectly.

Finding a way in proved more difficult. The walls around the complex were thick and tall. He had to walk for what felt like miles until he found an old gate. People were arguing there and rather than wait as he might have done if he were wearing his Dark Mage robes or the black leather armor, Max chugged one of Trina's flesh potions. Then he put up his visor and walked over to take a gander at whatever was going on.

There were two guards arguing with a short thin man who looked distraught.

"I'm sorry brother," The guard on the left said. They both wore bright shining scale mail with light tan cloaks. A long curved sword hung from each of their belts as well as a secondary curved dagger, yet each also held a spear with a thin piercing point.

Max couldn't help but think they were pretty well equipped for guarding the side gate of a monastery. His hunch was starting to feel even more likely.

"But... please. I must see her. I told you, his eminence has sent a gift," the small man said. His voice was strained, pleading.

"Do NOT lie to us," the other guard said. "We were told about you. Now begone, or you'll feel the bite of my blade!"

"I..." the man started to reply. Max could see he was trying to think of something else to say, some way to convince the guards.

"I said GO!" the second guard shouted as he kicked the man in his stomach causing him to double over. Then he pushed him into the dirt with his hands. Both guards laughed.

The small man's face was red with frustration and something else, maybe sadness, as he picked himself up and stumbled away. Max waited until he was out of eye shot of the guards and approached him. In his mind, there was never a more obvious side quest in the history of any game, ever. But even if it wasn't, even if this guy was just being turned away because he was crazy, Max could probably learn something useful.

"Hi," Max said, using a hand to make sure his helmet's visor was up.

The man was startled. “Stay away from me!” he said, until his eyes drifted down to the straight dagger and axe hanging at his waist. “You're not Clathian,” he said.

“That's true,” Max said. “I'm not from here. I'm a traveling... uh.. Freelancer.”

The man nodded, licking his lips. He still looked ill.

“Would you like a salve or something?” Max asked.

“No,” the man said, “I'll... I'll be fine. May the grace of the goddess be yours.”

Max assumed this was a way to end the conversation as the small man started to turn away.

“Wait,” he said. “Tell me what was going on over there... What is that place?”

The man paused, frowning. “What do you know of it?”

“I know you want to get in there,” Max said, “and that those guards are remarkably well equipped for an old monastery.”

“I... I'm sorry,” the man said, moving to leave again. “May her peace be upon you.”

“I could get you in there,” Max said. “If you tell me what's going on.”

That stopped him. His head turned.

“And you mean no harm?”

"No," Max said. "Anytime I can accomplish a goal with the minimum bloodshed, I do it," he said. Not strictly true, especially lately, but hey, he'd been doing his best.

"Why have you come here?"

Best to be honest, he thought. "I'm looking for someone, a woman. I believe she might be here."

The man turned around, sighing. "You have come to the right place. There are many women inside. It is a Shalwal, a place for women to be purified in the light of the goddess. I too have come to find someone."

Max nodded. "I'm M.... Melvin," he said, realizing that if they had Arinna here, they probably knew his name. Actually, now that he thought about, there was probably a little poster with a skeleton on it pinned up in the square of every town everywhere.

"Muhmelvin?" the man replied, frowning. "Of what country is that?"

Max waved his hand. "It's not important."

"I must get inside," the man said.

"Ok," Max said, "Let's go then."

"But... But the guards..." the man said. "They're from an elite unit of Seyara, The Unyielding."

"I guess that's why they didn't let you in then, huh?" Max asked as they walked back toward the gate.

“Their power is unmatched, even their regular soldiers have been known to be level eight,” the man said.

“That high huh?” Max said, smiling. It was nice to feel his lips actually smile. “Well... I think we might be able to handle it.”

“No bloodshed?” the man asked.

“Yep,” Max replied.

The guards were still chatting with each other but stopped immediately when they saw Max and his new friend approaching. Spears came down and pointed at Max.

“You there!Approach no further!” one of them said.

Max paused about fifteen feet away. He looked back. The short guy was still behind him, but he sure didn't seem to want to be. His hands were shaking like crazy.

“It'll be fine,” Max said to him. “Relax.”

“You know that fool?” the other guard said. “Then you must leave, now.”

“Why is that?” Max asked. “He just wants to see his sister.”

“Leave!” the other guard said. “Or we will kill you.”

“I see,” Max said. “Well before I go, I have these extra hamburgers. I couldn't eat them all. Do you guys want them?”

One of the guards raised an eyebrow. “What's a hamberker?”

“Don't listen to him. It's a stupid trick of some kind,” the other guard said.

“No, seriously. They're delicious, here let me show you,” he said as he summoned five small bags into each of his hands. Both guards couldn't help but lean in involuntarily, even the skeptical one. There was just something about a new food that people couldn't resist, no matter what world you were in.

Max tossed the bags at the feet of the guards where they exploded into powder. Both guards looked surprised at first until their eyelids seemed to close on their own and they dropped with a clattering of metal and man. Then the snoring began.

“Sleep powder!” the man said. “How did you get so much of it?”

“I've got a source,” Max said as he took a key from the belt of one of the men. It was hidden under some thick sash that they both wore. Each was different though, as if the sashes had some kind of personal meaning, like a flag with a coat of arms, or the pattern on a kilt.

Max unlocked the gate and as soon as it opened the little man ran in, disappearing into the compound beyond.

“Not even a thank you,” Max said with a shrug.

He too entered, but with a little more care. Once he'd passed the wall, he walked slowly through what looked to be a series of dormitory buildings. They'd been built with style though, reminiscent a little of a cross between Chinese and Middle eastern design. Many were rounded with open courtyards and trellises. A lot of maintenance work was put into keeping this place perfect. That made it very different than the outside, which was just faceless, windowless walls. Inside it felt more like a Sultan's palace than a monastery, which was... concerning.

What was going on here? Man, if he only got one Gol for every time he'd thought that in this weird-ass world, he'd be a rich little bag of bones.

Max snuck around, trying to figure out where to go. The place was huge and every turn led to another building or a courtyard. Even weirder, all of them were filled with young women who wore the same simple tan dress with no ornamentation. They all had short hair too, cut high and tight... It was weird. At first he thought they just had a bunch of thin guys doing their grounds-keeping for them, until he heard them talking. They talked quietly, whispering, like they were afraid to be overheard.

He was about to give up and just ask one of the girls, when he heard men shouting.

MAX RAN down a long open corridor lined with trellises covered with an odd shaped red flower until he saw men running in the distance. Guards, three of them. They went from his left to right down at the end of the hall.

He cut through a low arch in the middle of the trellis and emerged in a wide open lawn with a few well manicured trees. There was a slope in the distance and a cool breeze blowing that made him want to take off his helmet and feel it in his hair, while he still had some. He didn't though, instead he moved to his right, careful to remain nonchalant to keep from attracting any unnecessary attention.

The shouting was coming from down the slope. Max approached, cautiously. He saw the small man from before in the distance, crouched behind one of the women and he watched as a large crossbow bolt shot in from the left, hitting the man in the center of his his back with an audible thump. The man slumped to the ground but his hands were still reaching toward the woman.

Men followed the bolt, guards. They had spears that they used to impale the little man, multiple times, before pausing to talk to the young woman. Then they dragged the corpse away, leaving the woman there alone.

Max stood under the shade of a tree nearby. Should he have intervened? Maybe, but the attacks had been too quick, he wouldn't have saved the man, just made everyone aware he was here. He could handle three level eight guards, but twenty-three? Maybe not.

Oddly, the girl hadn't moved. She was just sitting there under the tree, holding a little cup.

He should leave her be. Yeah... She was probably traumatized.

Max turned in a circle, scanning around. There were a few other young women nearby, as well as some creepy looking guys in long robes who seemed to be monitoring them, maybe a little too closely. Max was starting to hate this place. It would go on the list of places to eradicate once they found Arinna.

He sighed. Time to head back.

Max turned to go when a hand gripped his elbow. He turned.

There she was.

All this time, all this searching and now Arinna stood before him. Sure, her hair had been cut short and maybe even bleached somehow, but the face was the same, the eyes were the same. The sense of relief was like a flood, filling him with emotion that welled up at the corners of his eyes.

"The goddess is great," she said, looking up at him.

Max choked back the tears in his eyes. "Huh?" he replied.

She frowned. Oh... this must be one of those call and response things religions were so fond of.

"The goddess is great," he said. Yes... yes she was. "I'm sorry, you startled me."

Her expression softened. "I see," she said, smiling a little, pulling a tiny piece of her very short bangs from her eyes.

The teeth! Her vampire fangs were gone! Was it her then? Yes. It was. Absolutely. They'd done this to her. Somehow they'd changed her teeth. Even her skin tone seemed more rosy and normal looking, more human.

"Are you looking for someone?" she asked.

"Actually, I am," he said. "She's important to me. I was told I might find her here."

"Is it... your wife?" she asked, her eyes lowering.

"No," Max replied.

"Oh!" she said. "Tell me her name and what she looks like and I'll see if I can help you."

Max looked at her. It was taking everything he had not to reach out and grab her and run out of this place but he couldn't, he knew that. She would freak out. If she hadn't already recognized him by now, then her memory might be gone completely. Though, it had been forever since they'd seen each other. Well... no actually, It hadn't. That night was only a few weeks ago.

He touched his face. Was there still skin? There was.

Arinna laughed. "Something wrong with your face?"

Max smiled. "You could say that. Uh... can I ask what you do here?"

"I am nokara," she said, her eyes dropping to her feet. The incredible confidence from their first meeting seemed gone, replaced by a kind of enduring sadness. Even when she smiled, he felt it lurking in the background like a taint in a well. "I am bound to this temple."

“Yeah?” he asked. “You seem… maybe a little down.”

“No,” she replied. “Cerathia is god and I am her servant, wrong feelings are a sin. I do not have them.”

Max's lips pressed together. No. No more. “I came here for you. We have to go. One of the important guys here wants to see you. They told me.”

She frowned. “But… “

“What's your name?” Max asked.

“Mishina,” she said.

“That's exactly who I'm looking for,” he said. Then he held out his hand. “Will you come with me?”

She looked down. “I… I shouldn't. I can't…”

“Please?”

“No…” she shook her head. “There is work. I have temple work to do and… and… if I do it well.”

Max re-extended his hand. “Come with me. Everything will be fine. I promise. We'll make sure your chores are taken care of.”

“I… No…” she said.

Max sighed. “Well… there is one thing.”

She frowned, looking up. “What?”

Voices were yelling behind Max, deep voices. This did not bode well.

"I have something for you... but I can't give it to you here. Come with me to the roof. Will you?"

"You can come right right back," he said.

She nodded and finally took his hand. "This way," she said. "We'll go to the third tower."

She led him through two more tunnel-like corridors with flower trellises and up three flights of stairs before they slipped into a thick circular building with a high arched doorway. Then they ascended a spiral stair that swirled its way up and up before finally they reached a door.

Arinna pulled on the lever but it didn't move. She turned back, looking crestfallen. "It's locked... this was foolish... I should get back."

Max stepped forward and smashed a foot into the door. It popped open with a crisp crack.

"Looks open to me," he said.

She laughed. One thing that hadn't changed from before. Her laugh. It was the same, it made his heart jump like a fish in lake. They stepped out into a small circular area ringed with crenelations of stone. There was a pole with a brown flag. It had a single white ten pointed star in the center where the topmost point was extra big, but the bottom most was extra small. There had to be some meaning to it, but Max had no idea what it was.

"Is that... is that the ocean?" she asked, looking out to the east.

"It is," Max said as he used the mirror to signal. It wasn't hard to find the Midnight. The Kestrian patrol ship was quite a bit smaller than the merchant ships surrounding it. It started moving immediately.

Arinna went to the edge, putting her hands on the stone as the wind blew through her hair.

"I have a question," Max said.

She turned. "Yes?"

"Does the name Arinna mean anything to you?"

Her lip quivered. It looked like she was trying to swallow something bitter. "No," she said.

"I know that's not true," he said. "Here."

He held out the letter. "A friend said this might help you."

The moment she touched it, the seal broke and the letter opened. Arinna seemed reticent to read the words inside but her eyes finally lowered to the paper in her hands. Tears welled up.

"No!" she said. "No!"

Below Max could hear shouting.

Shit. Someone must have seen them come up here.

Arinna tried to throw the letter away, but it wouldn't go, it stuck to her hand like it had been glued there flapping in the breeze as she shook it, her face reddening, tears rolling down her cheeks.

“You are Arinna,” he said. “I don't know what it says but that letter is yours...”

She was sobbing now and collapsed to the ground. “But... no... I don't want it...why?”

Max sighed. The boots were getting closer now, any moment they'd be at the top.

“Sometimes we have to do something we don't feel ready for,” he said. “Believe me, I know. I've traveled this world looking for you. I didn't think I was ready for any of it, but I was. Please... come with me. Be free.”

He reached down, holding out his hand. This time she took it and stood and embraced him, wrapping her arms around his human body.

“I... I think I remember you,” she said. “You made fun of Vishellus's eye.”

“Yeah,” Max said. “I did.”

The ship approached from the left bringing the rope ladder with it.

“You have a ship?”

“I do,” he replied.

He sent her up the ladder first and relished giving the finger to the guards that appeared at the top of the tower. Until one of them pulled out a crossbow and put a bolt in his right leg.

24 damage received.

"Argh!" Max yelled, dragging himself up. "Sometimes I really hate this place."

When Max made it up the ladder, instead of finding Arinna standing or sitting, he found her doubled up on the floor, curled into fetal position.

"Are you on board?" Trina yelled from the bridge.

"Yes!" he replied. He heard Trina tell Tela to get them out of here and felt as the ship rapidly changed direction. Then there was a thunderous boom and the entire ship shook.

"What was that?!" Max yelled as he pulled up and ladder and closed the lower hatch. He turned around to see Arinna still on the floor. Scruff was next to her.

"Why is she like this?" Max asked. "Did you do something to her?"

Scruff shook all his tentacles angrily.

"Ok... Sorry, sorry. I'm a little stressed."

There was another boom and the ship shook a second time.

Max bent down next to Arinna. "Hold on Ok? I'm going to check on stuff and I'll be right back with a doctor."

Max ran to the bridge. "What the hell is going on?"

"Every ship in the Clathian navy is chasing us and shooting us!" Trina said. "Tela, can't we go any faster?"

"We are already going as fast as we can!" Tela replied cheerily. "Their ships are slow. We should out run them soon."

There was another boom to their right and the ship shook again.

"What the hell spell is that?" Max asked.

"I don't know!" Trina said. "I'm not a mage I'm a doctor!"

Max's eyebrows went up. "Oh... Arinna's not feeling well."

"Arinna is here?!?" Trina said, eyes wide. "You found her?!"

"Yes!" Max said as his eyebrows slid down his face, running into his nose. Uh oh... his flesh was melting away. The potion had run out. "Come on!"

"Your face... uh..."

"I know, Trina!" Max said as he ran into the back with her. "I thought you said these potions lasted all day!"

"Yeah well... Potion making is as much an art as a science sometimes and some of it is luck," she replied.

Max returned to the bottom hatch room, but Arinna wasn't there. He found Scruff in the hall heading to the rear. The crawler pointed to the back of the ship and Max ran through, coming to the cargo bay just as Arinna pulled the lever catch and the door dropped open revealing pure blue ocean below.

"ARINNA!" Max screamed. "STOP!"

She was walking toward the back. Trina ran by Max and dived to tackle her but Arinna whipped around and with a vicious roundhouse kick smashed Trina into the side of the bay. Trina slumped, not moving.

"Arinna!" Max shouted at her.

Her body was contorting unnaturally before him, twisting like a marionette in the hands of a demented child.

"ARINNA!" he screamed again, reaching for her hand.

Then she turned and looked at him, her face filled with a wicked snarl. A golden glow pulsed from her eyes.

"She's mine," Arinna said, but the voice was not her own. Her body convulsed again, shaking violently as if a fierce battle were being waged inside her. For a second her face relaxed and her eyes seemed to focus on him.

"Max..." she said and reached for him before something jerked her one last time, pulling her out of the cargo bay.

Max didn't waste any time.

He ran to the edge and he jumped.

THE END

Bone knight book 6: As we've learned from Raeg's experience, the obstacles never stop showing up, even when you're dead. What will become of Max and Arinna now that they've taken the plunge together? Max's journey won't be simple or easy, but he won't be denied. He'll go to any length to accomplish his goal, earning his most powerful class yet. The question is, will it be enough?

. . .

AN AGONIZING DAY and A Dread Knight is available now on Amazon.

MAILING LIST

If you haven't already, be sure to join Tim Paulson's mailing list so you can hear about new releases and free giveaways before anyone else. Just drop by www.paulsonwriter.com and fill out the form.

Thank you for reading!

ACKNOWLEDGMENTS

Thank you to everyone who helped make this novel possible but especially my extraordinary wife and sons. Additional thanks to the following invaluable people, places, things, creatures, artificial beings and human like entities:

Uncle Dogster
Blizzardlizard
Milo
Mary
Metallica
Andy Rooney
Brittney
Spiders